2nd Gr.
B + N

W9-BZQ-424

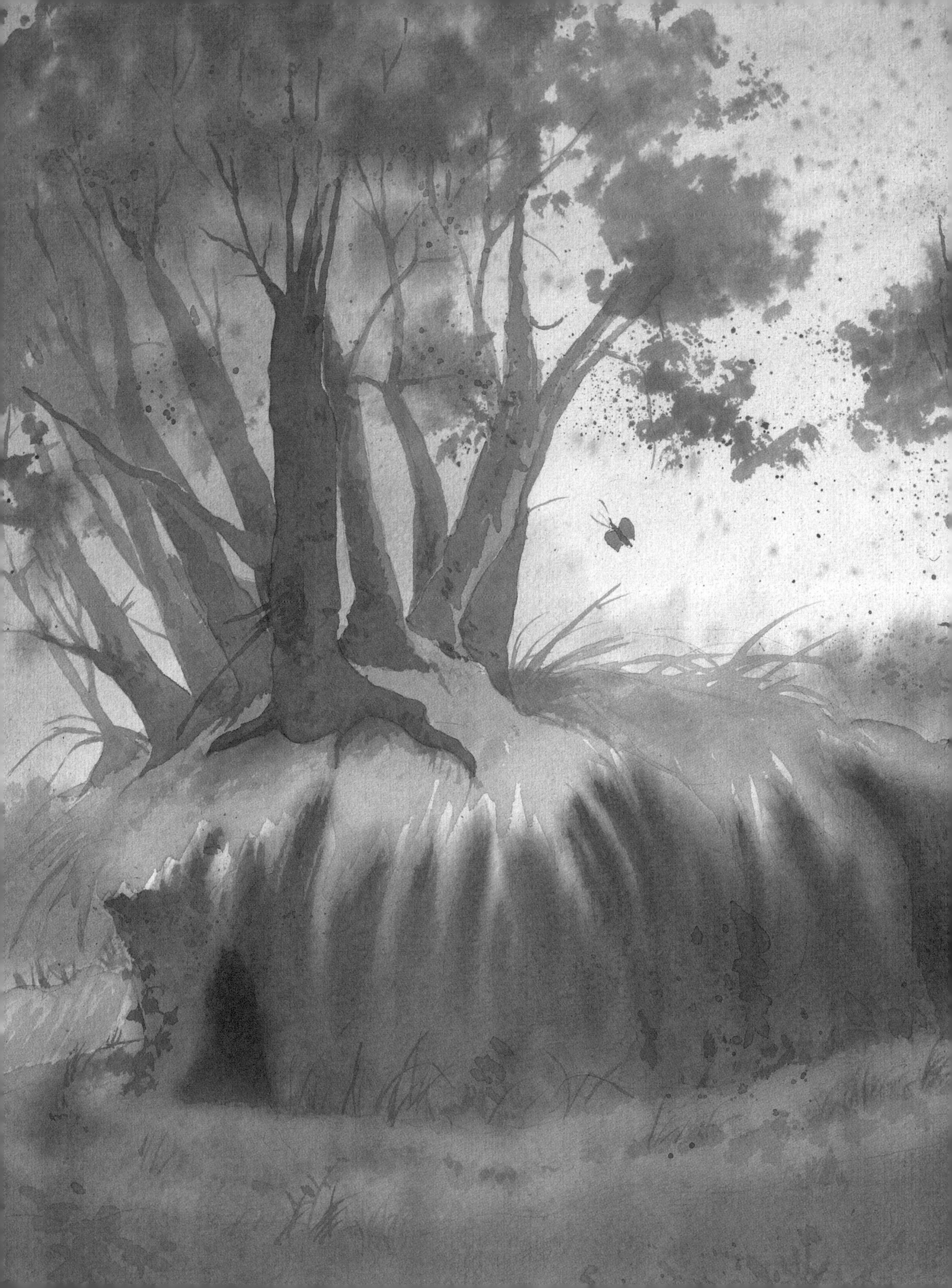

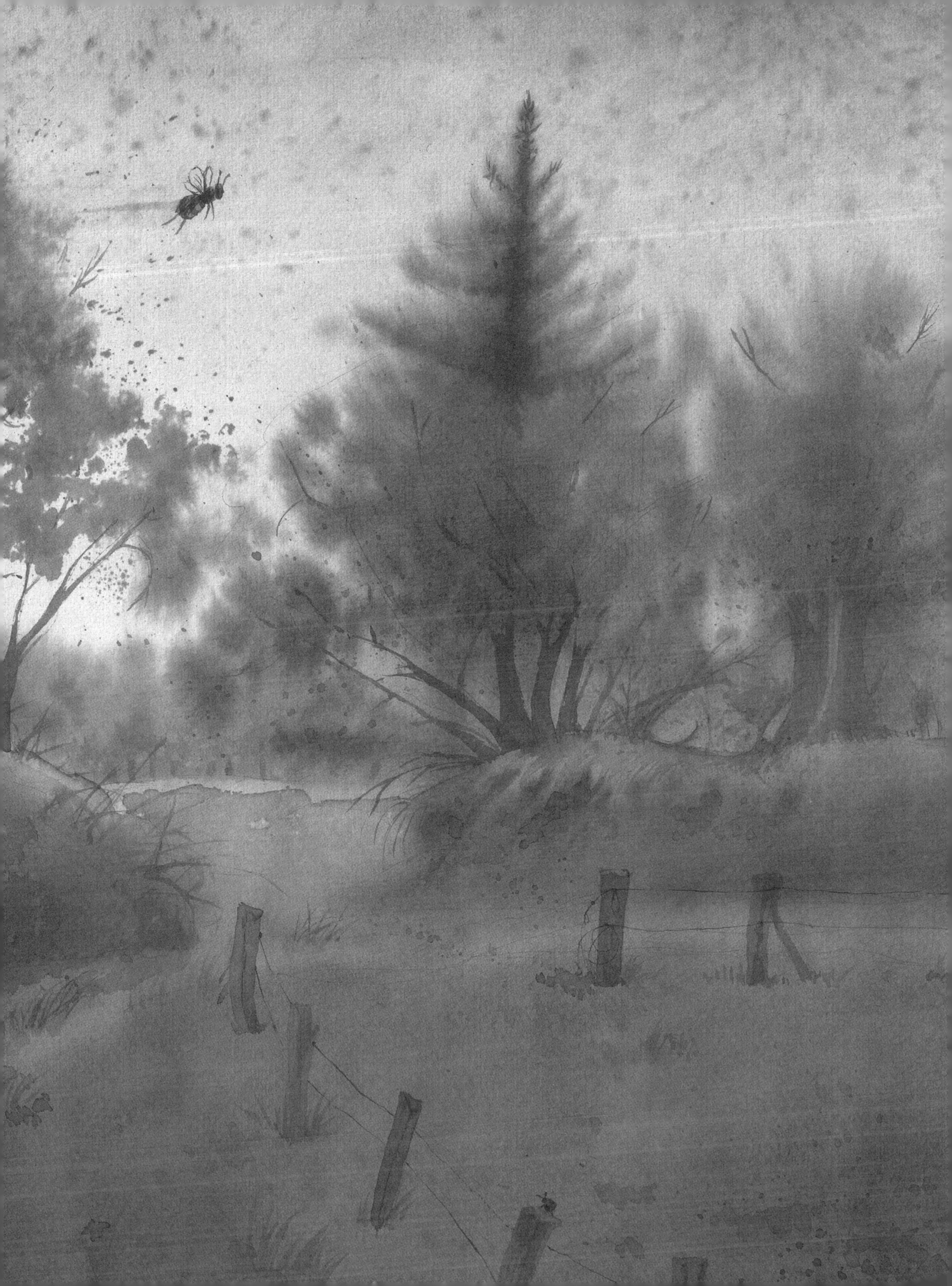

MR. BADGER AND MRS. FOX #5

THE CARNIVAL

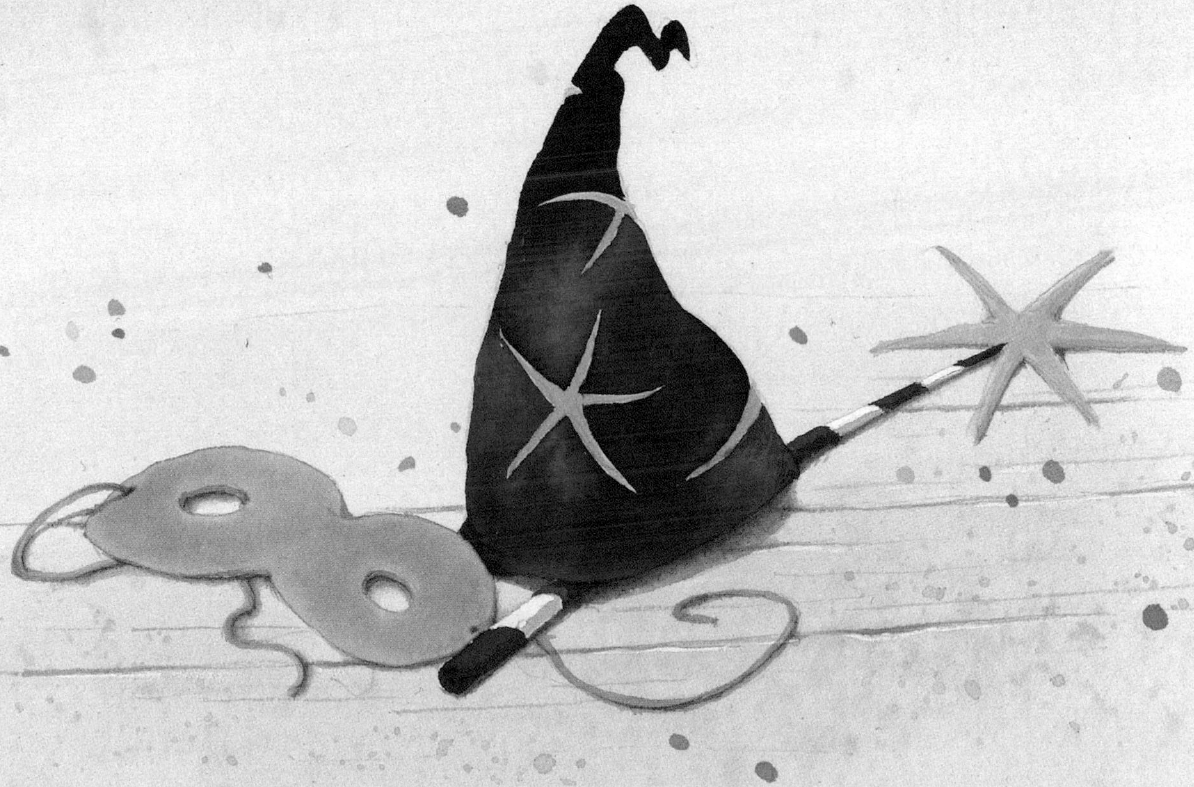

Brigitte LUCIANI & Eve THARLET

Graphic Universe™ • Minneapolis

To my daughters . . .
—B.L.

To my boys . . .
—E.T.

Story by Brigitte Luciani
Art by Eve Tharlet
Translation by Carol Klio Burrell

First American edition published in 2014 by Graphic Universe™.
Published by arrangement with MEDIATOON LICENSING - France.

Monsieur Blaireau et Madame Renarde
5/Le Carnaval
© DARGAUD 2012 - Tharlet & Luciani
www.dargaud.com

Graphic Universe™
A division of Lerner Publishing Group, Inc.
241 First Avenue North
Minneapolis, MN 55401 USA

For reading levels and more information, look up this title at www.lernerbooks.com.

Library of Congress Cataloging-in-Publication Data

Luciani, Brigitte.
[Carnaval. English]
The carnival / by Brigitte Luciani ; illustrated by Eve Tharlet ;
translation by Carol Klio Burrell. — First American edition.
p.   cm. — (Mr. Badger and Mrs. Fox ; #5)
Summary: After a long, cold winter, the foxes and badgers decide to
put on a carnival to chase away their grumpiness.
ISBN 978-1-4677-4203-0 (lib. bdg. : alk. paper)
ISBN 978-1-4677-4205-4 (eBook)
1. Graphic novels. [1. Graphic novels. 2. Carnivals—Fiction. 3. Stepfamilies—Fiction.
4. Grandparents—Fiction. 5. Badgers—Fiction. 6. Foxes—Fiction.]
I. Tharlet, Eve, illustrator. II. Burrell, Carol Klio, translator. III. Title.
PZ7.7.L83Car 2014
741.5—dc23   2013040909

Manufactured in the United States of America
1 - CG - 7/15/14

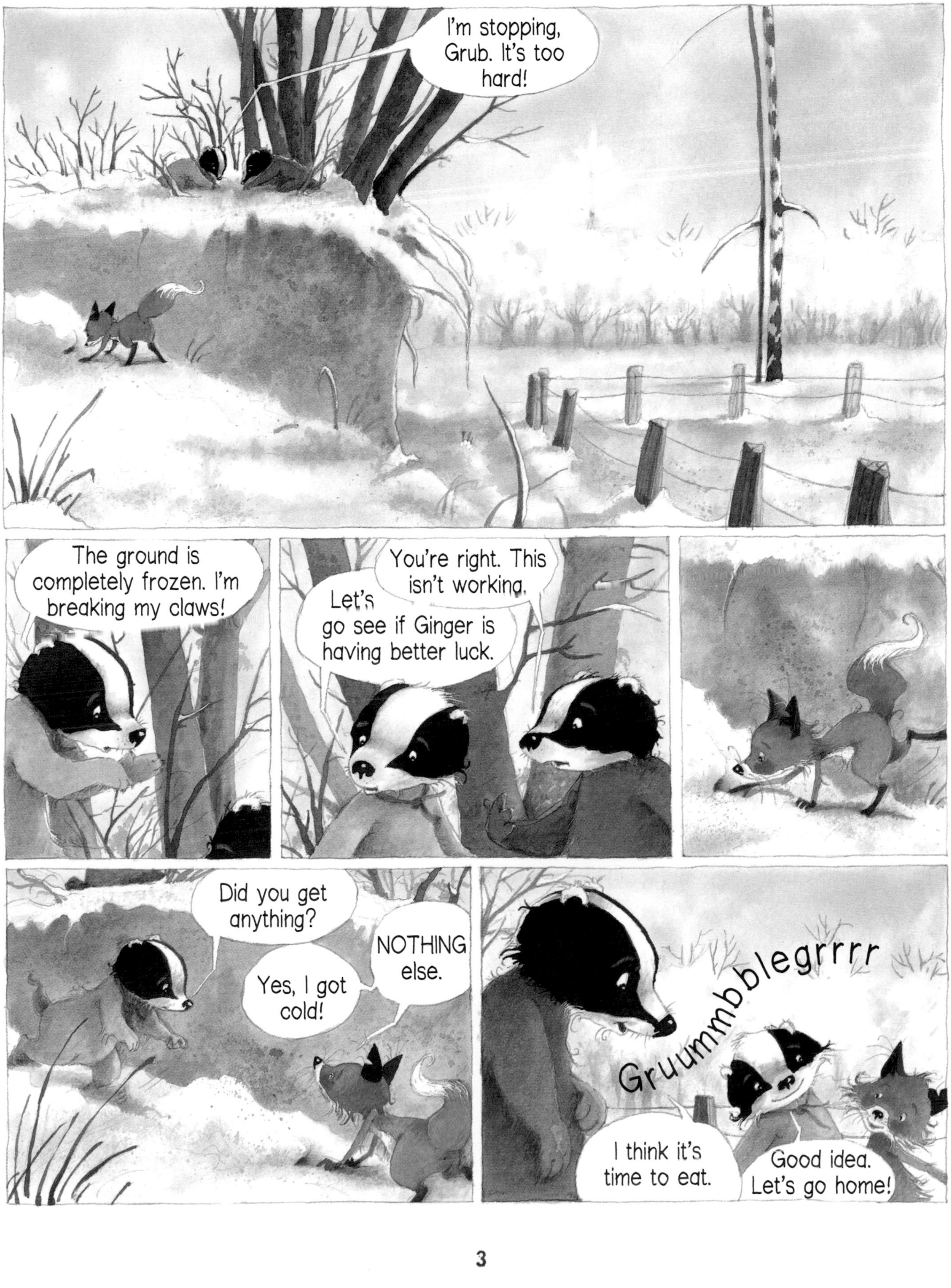
I'm stopping, Grub. It's too hard!
The ground is completely frozen. I'm breaking my claws!
You're right. This isn't working.
Let's go see if Ginger is having better luck.
Did you get anything?
Yes, I got cold!
NOTHING else.
Gruummbblegrrrr
I think it's time to eat.
Good idea. Let's go home!

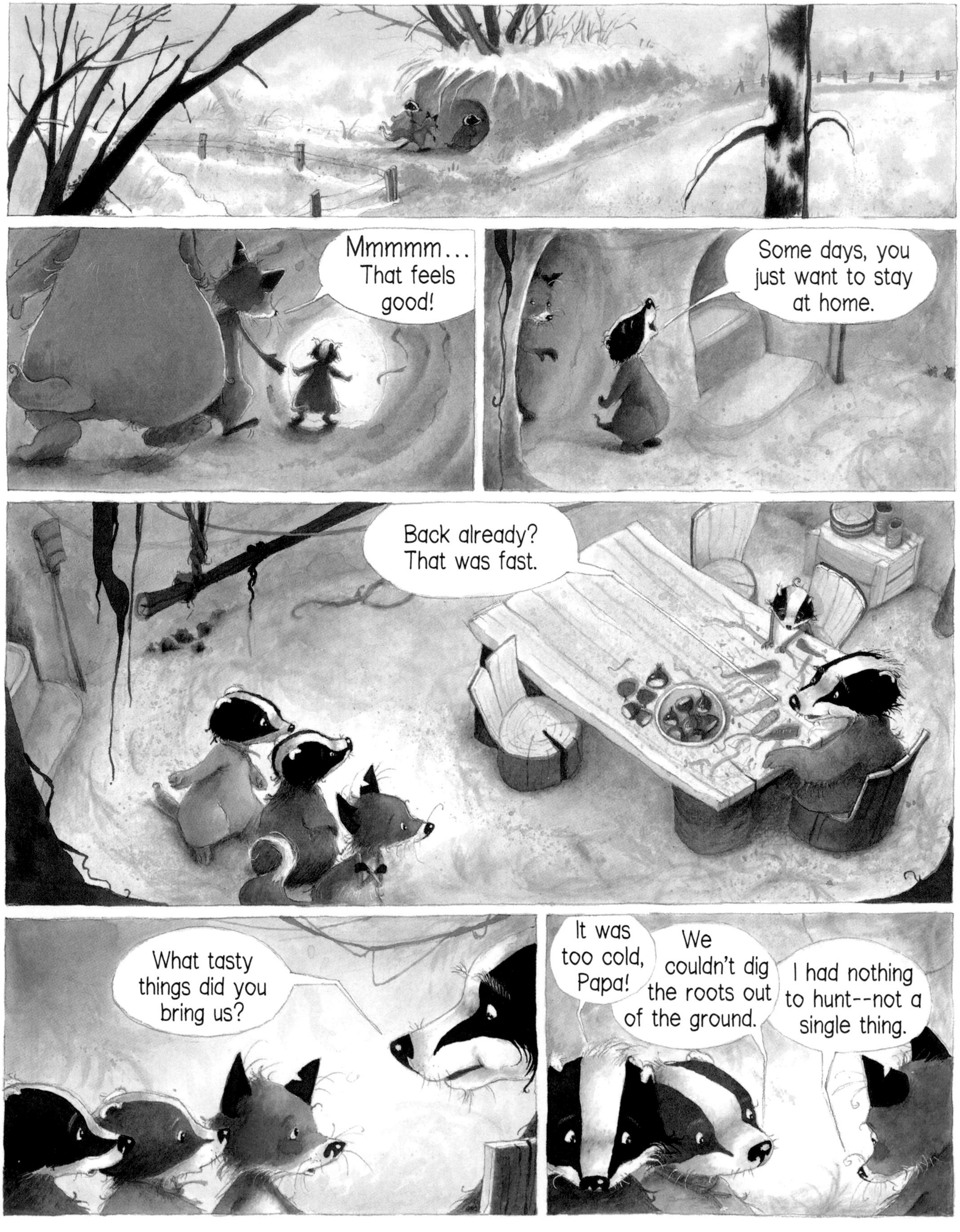

Mmmmm... That feels good!
Some days, you just want to stay at home.
Back already? That was fast.
What tasty things did you bring us?
It was too cold, Papa!
We couldn't dig the roots out of the ground.
I had nothing to hunt--not a single thing.

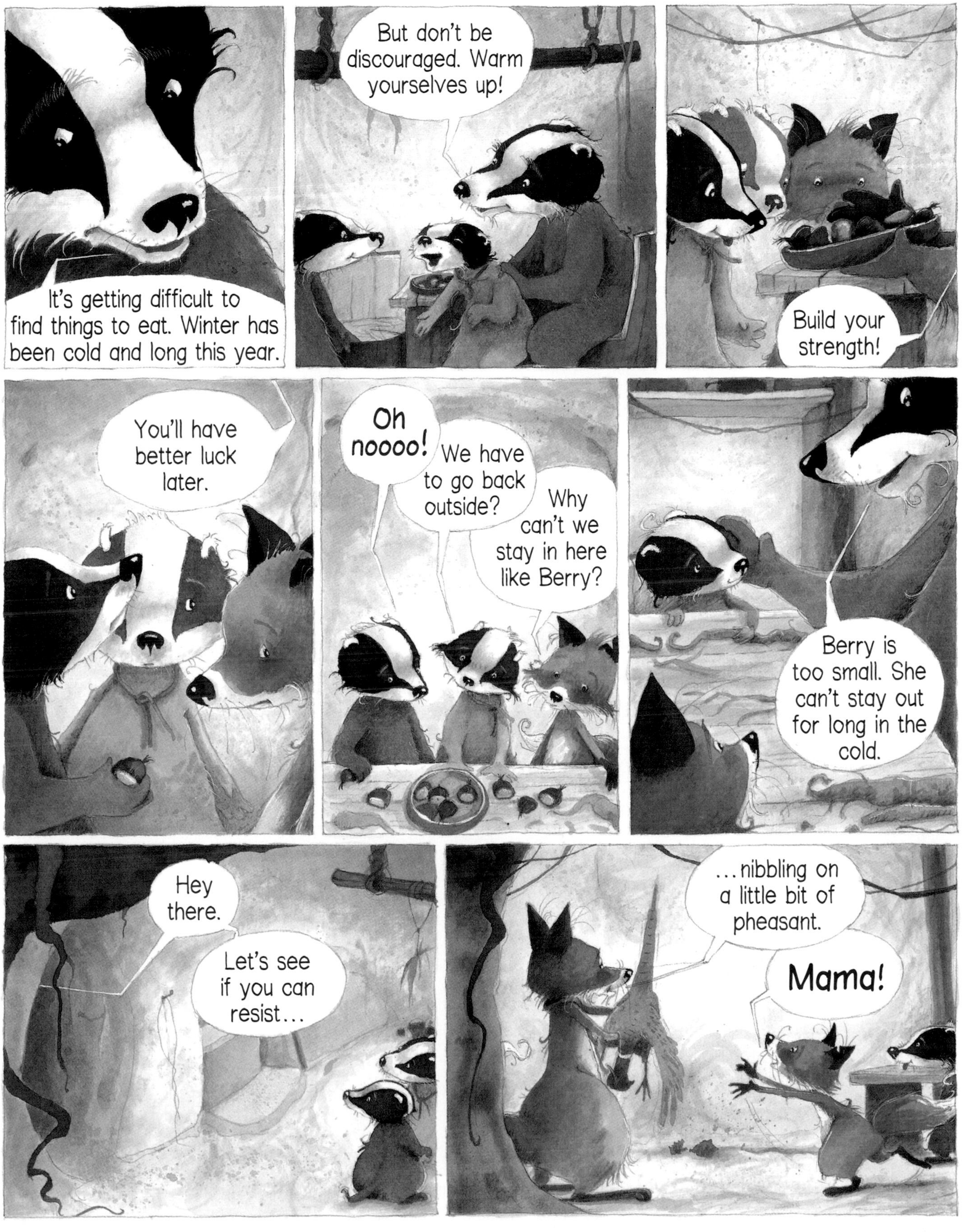
It's getting difficult to find things to eat. Winter has been cold and long this year.
But don't be discouraged. Warm yourselves up!
Build your strength!
You'll have better luck later.
Oh noooo!
We have to go back outside?
Why can't we stay in here like Berry?
Berry is too small. She can't stay out for long in the cold.
Hey there.
Let's see if you can resist...
...nibbling on a little bit of pheasant.
Mama!

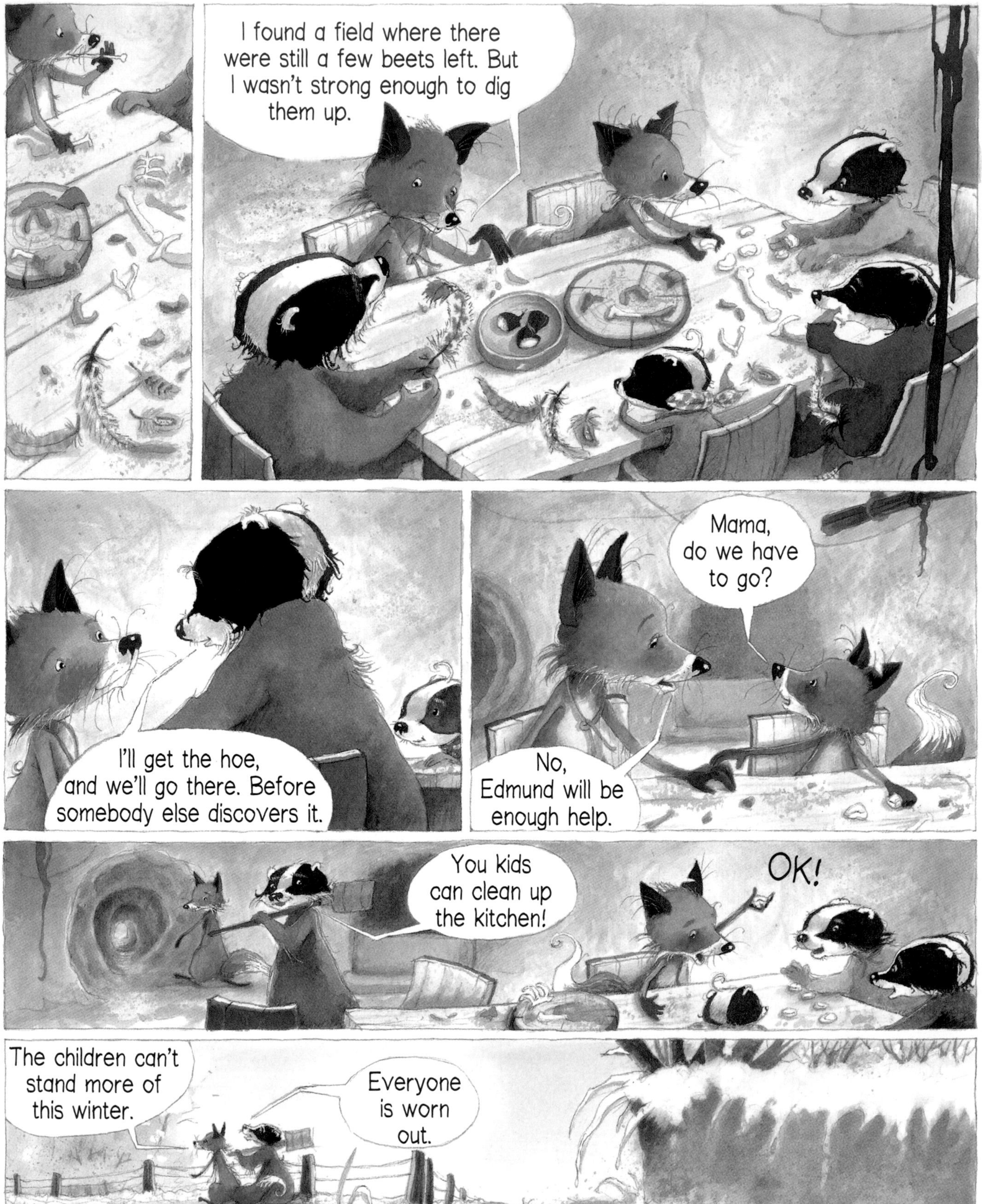
I found a field where there were still a few beets left. But I wasn't strong enough to dig them up.
I'll get the hoe, and we'll go there. Before somebody else discovers it.
Mama, do we have to go?
No, Edmund will be enough help.
You kids can clean up the kitchen!
OK!
The children can't stand more of this winter.
Everyone is worn out.

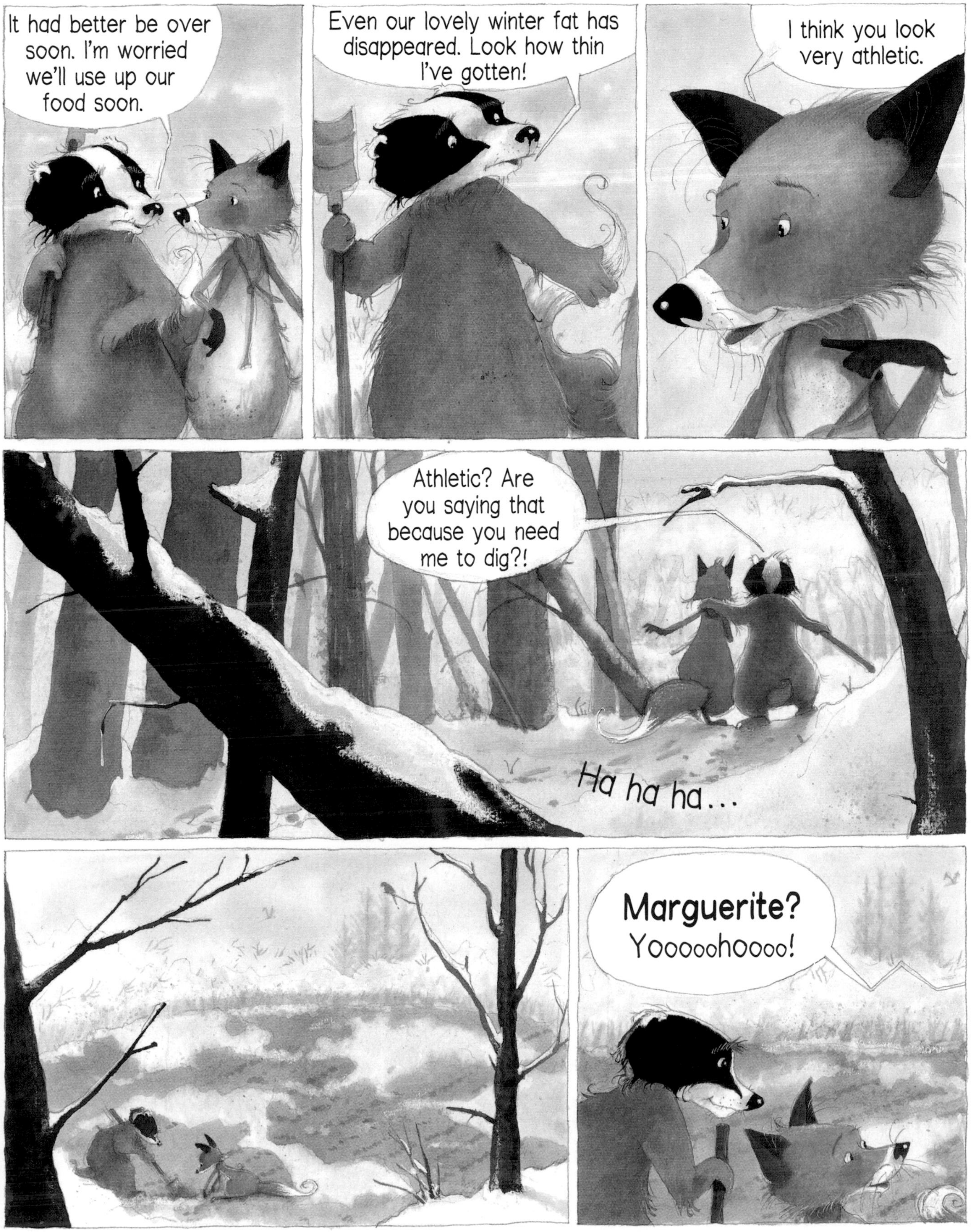
It had better be over soon. I'm worried we'll use up our food soon.
Even our lovely winter fat has disappeared. Look how thin I've gotten!
I think you look very athletic.
Athletic? Are you saying that because you need me to dig?!
Ha ha ha...
Marguerite? Yooooohoooo!

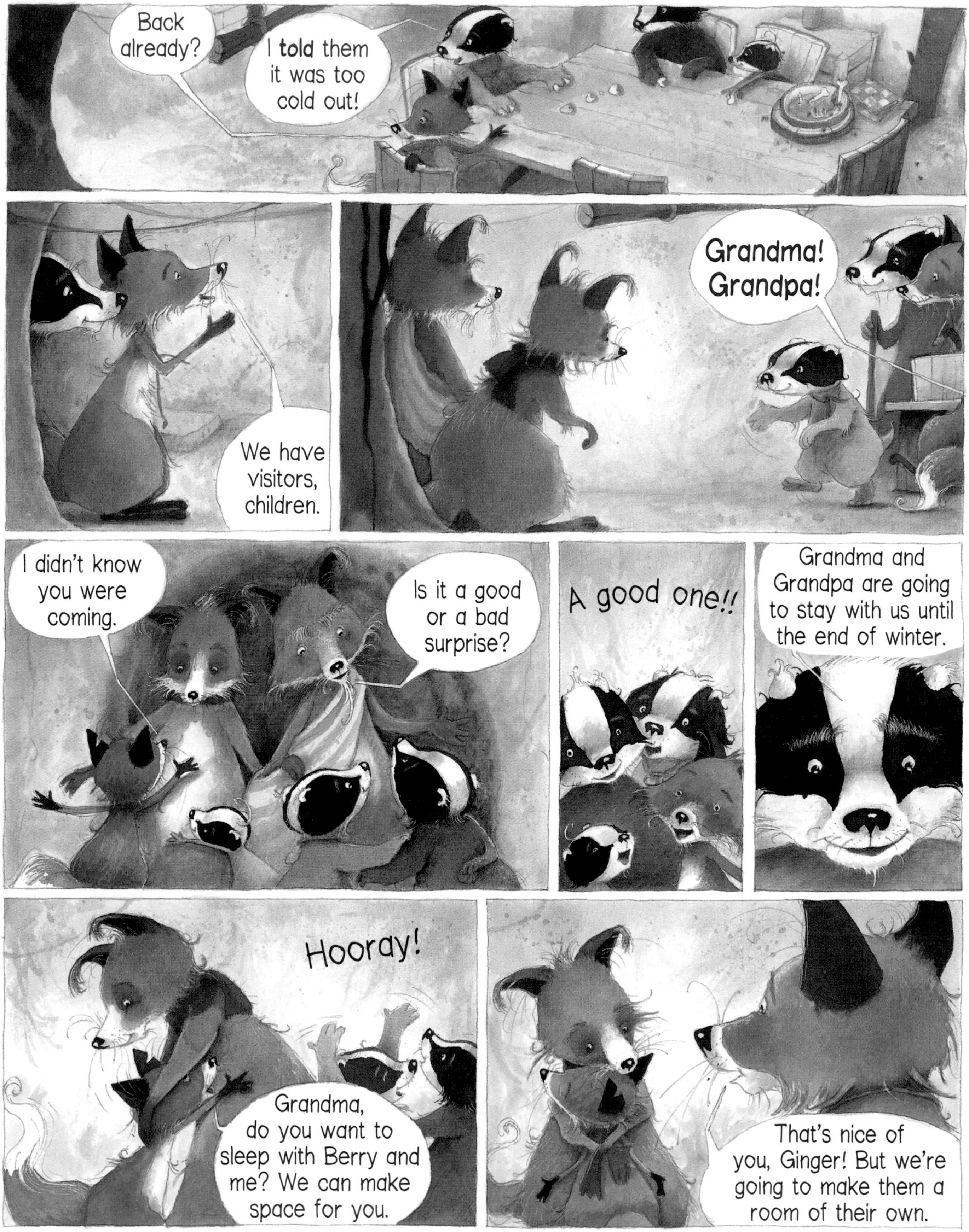
Back already?
I **told** them it was too cold out!
We have visitors, children.
Grandma! Grandpa!
I didn't know you were coming.
Is it a good or a bad surprise?
A good one!!
Grandma and Grandpa are going to stay with us until the end of winter.
Hooray!
Grandma, do you want to sleep with Berry and me? We can make space for you.
That's nice of you, Ginger! But we're going to make them a room of their own.

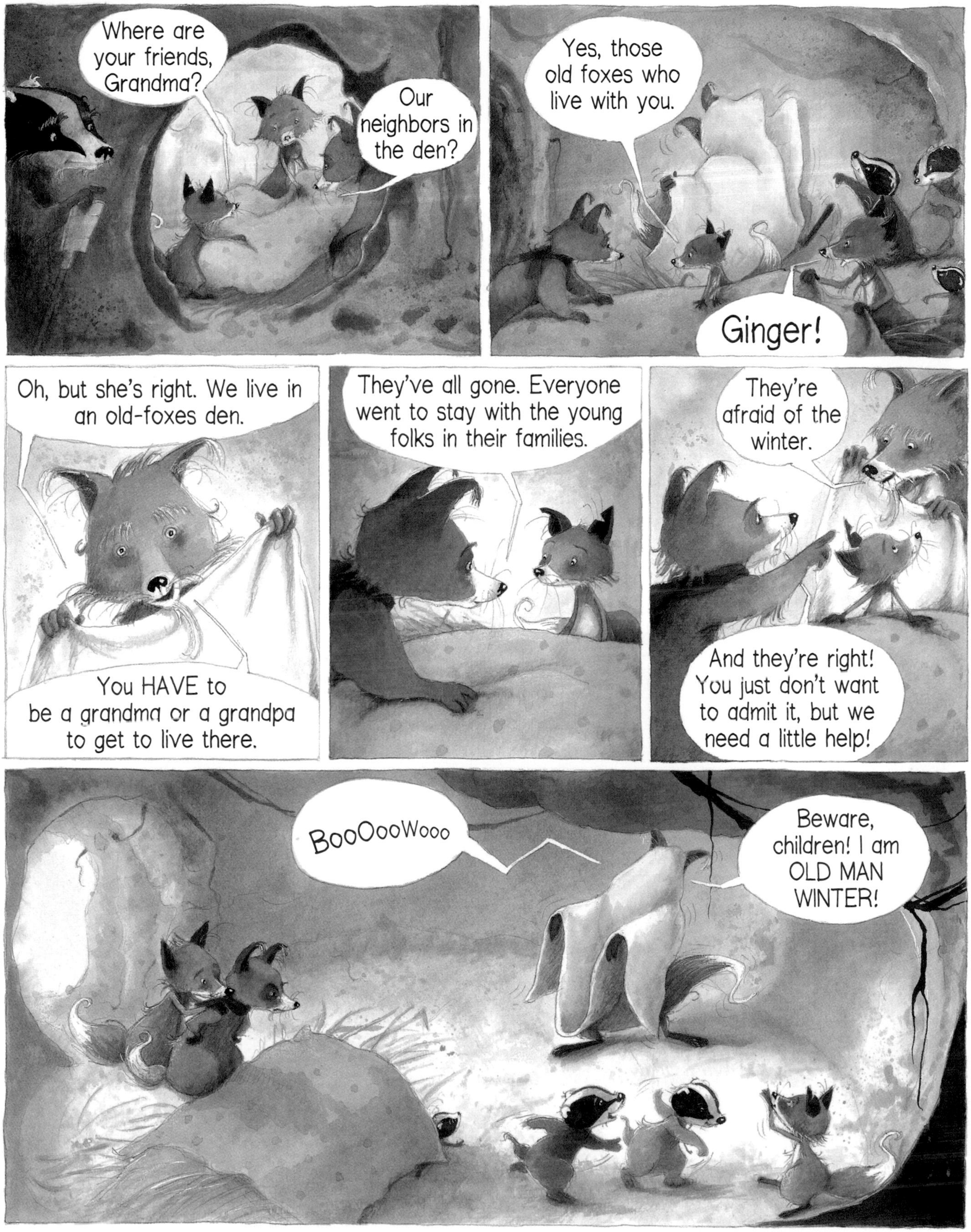
Where are your friends, Grandma?
Our neighbors in the den?
Yes, those old foxes who live with you.
Ginger!
Oh, but she's right. We live in an old-foxes den.
You HAVE to be a grandma or a grandpa to get to live there.
They've all gone. Everyone went to stay with the young folks in their families.
They're afraid of the winter.
And they're right! You just don't want to admit it, but we need a little help!
BooOooWooo
Beware, children! I am OLD MAN WINTER!

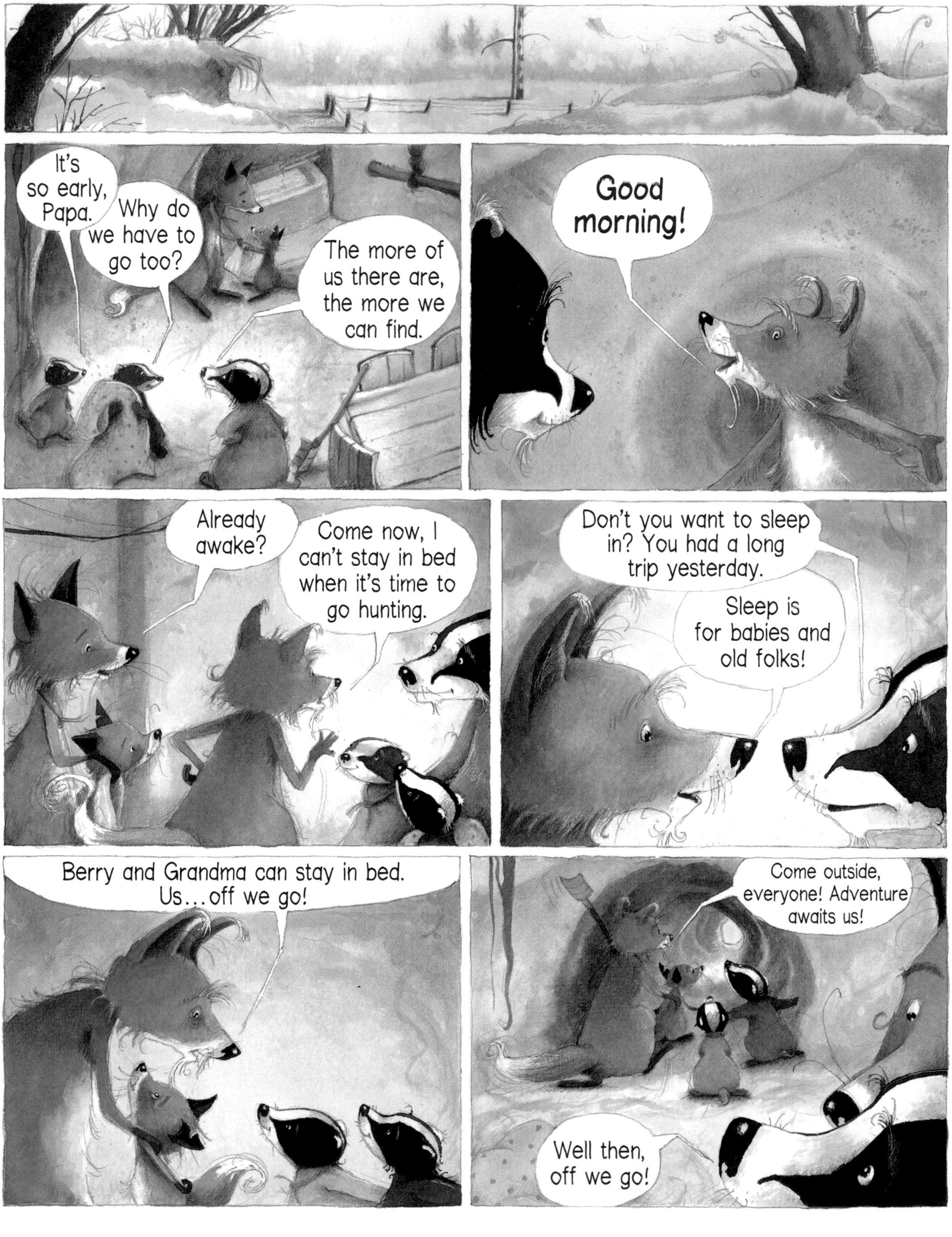
It's so early, Papa.
Why do we have to go too?
The more of us there are, the more we can find.
Good morning!
Already awake?
Come now, I can't stay in bed when it's time to go hunting.
Don't you want to sleep in? You had a long trip yesterday.
Sleep is for babies and old folks!
Berry and Grandma can stay in bed. Us...off we go!
Come outside, everyone! Adventure awaits us!
Well then, off we go!

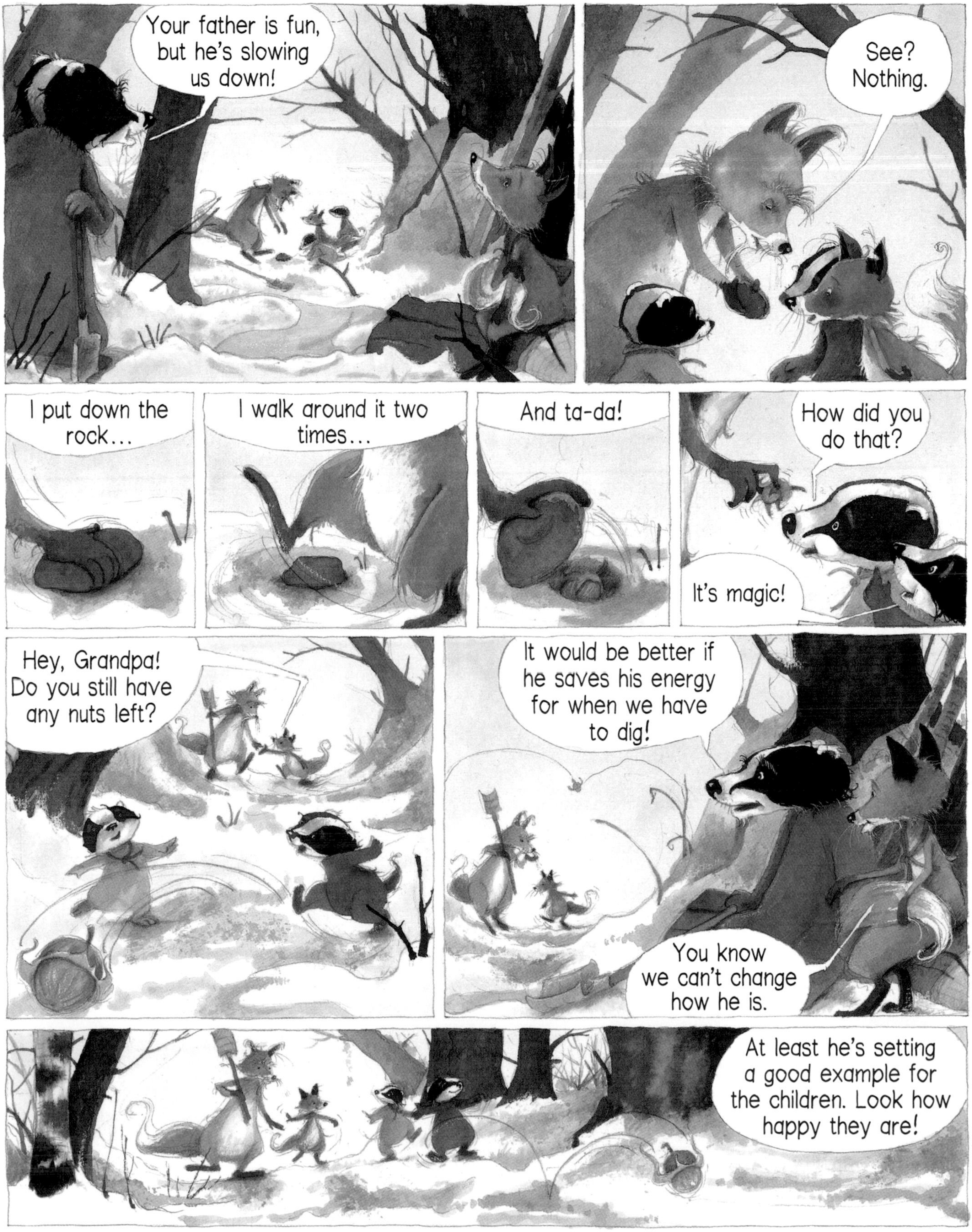
Your father is fun, but he's slowing us down!
See? Nothing.
I put down the rock...
I walk around it two times...
And ta-da!
How did you do that?
It's magic!
Hey, Grandpa! Do you still have any nuts left?
It would be better if he saves his energy for when we have to dig!
You know we can't change how he is.
At least he's setting a good example for the children. Look how happy they are!

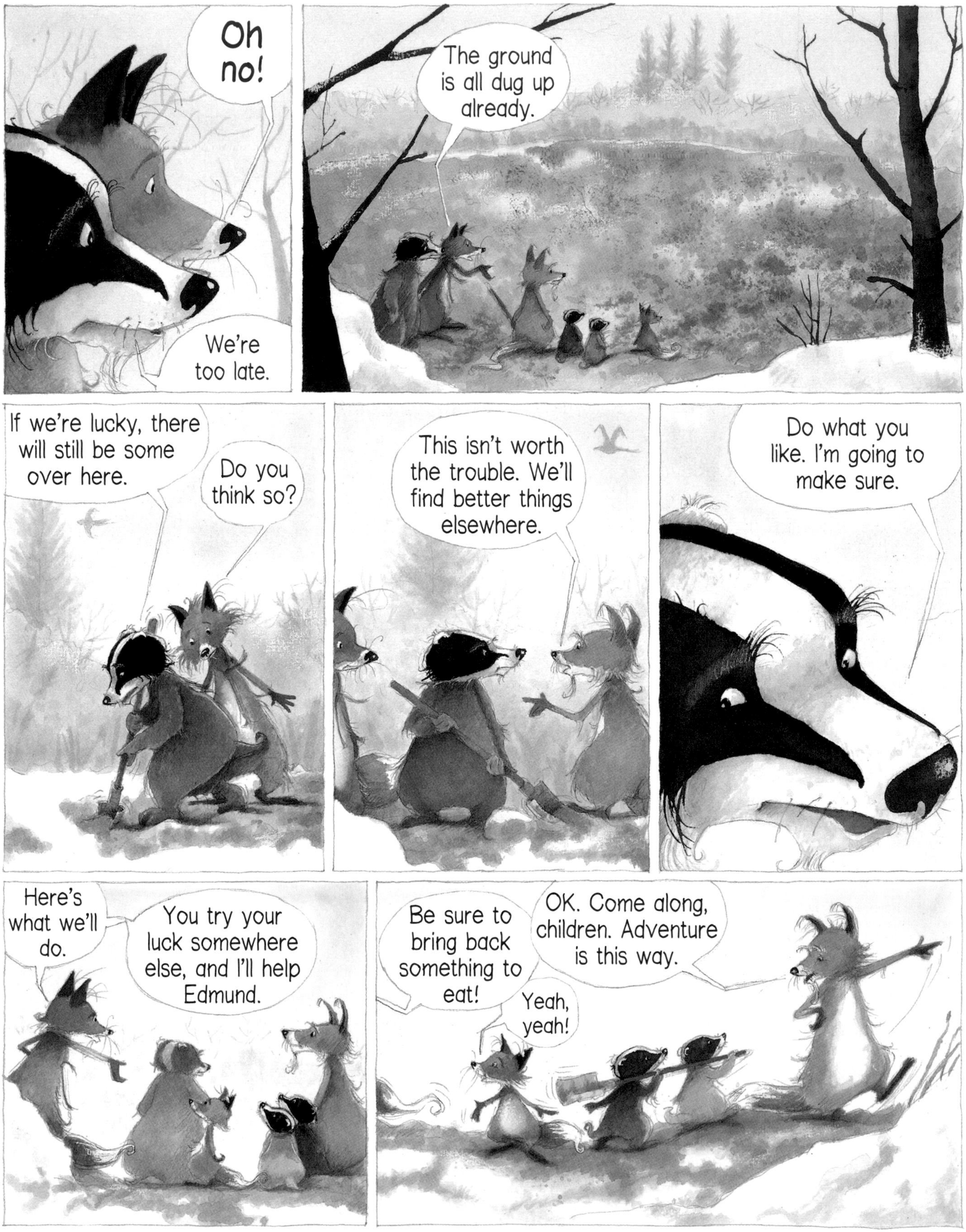
Oh no!
We're too late.
The ground is all dug up already.
If we're lucky, there will still be some over here.
Do you think so?
This isn't worth the trouble. We'll find better things elsewhere.
Do what you like. I'm going to make sure.
Here's what we'll do.
You try your luck somewhere else, and I'll help Edmund.
Be sure to bring back something to eat!
OK. Come along, children. Adventure is this way.
Yeah, yeah!

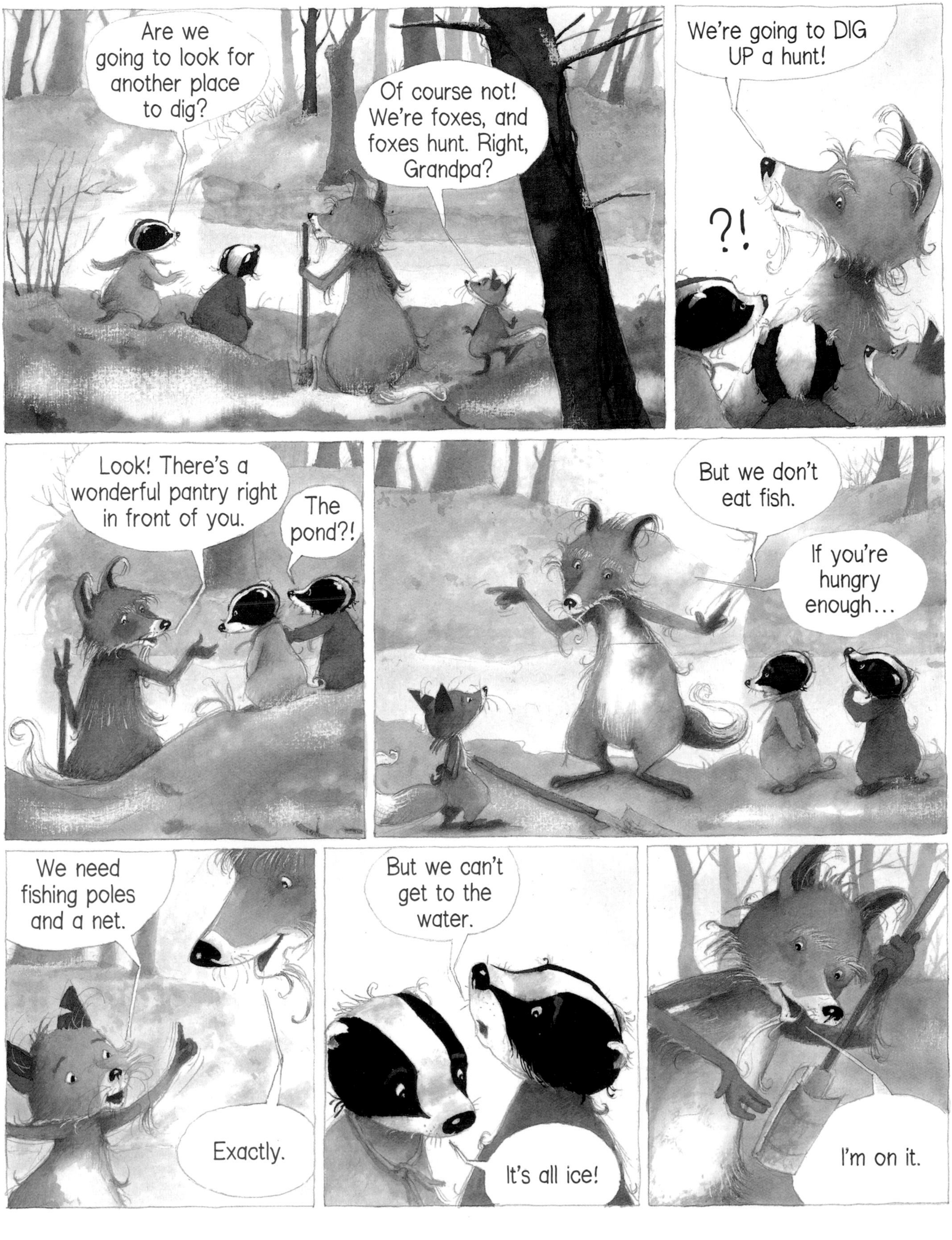
Are we going to look for another place to dig?
Of course not! We're foxes, and foxes hunt. Right, Grandpa?
We're going to DIG UP a hunt!
?!
Look! There's a wonderful pantry right in front of you.
The pond?!
But we don't eat fish.
If you're hungry enough...
We need fishing poles and a net.
Exactly.
But we can't get to the water.
It's all ice!
I'm on it.

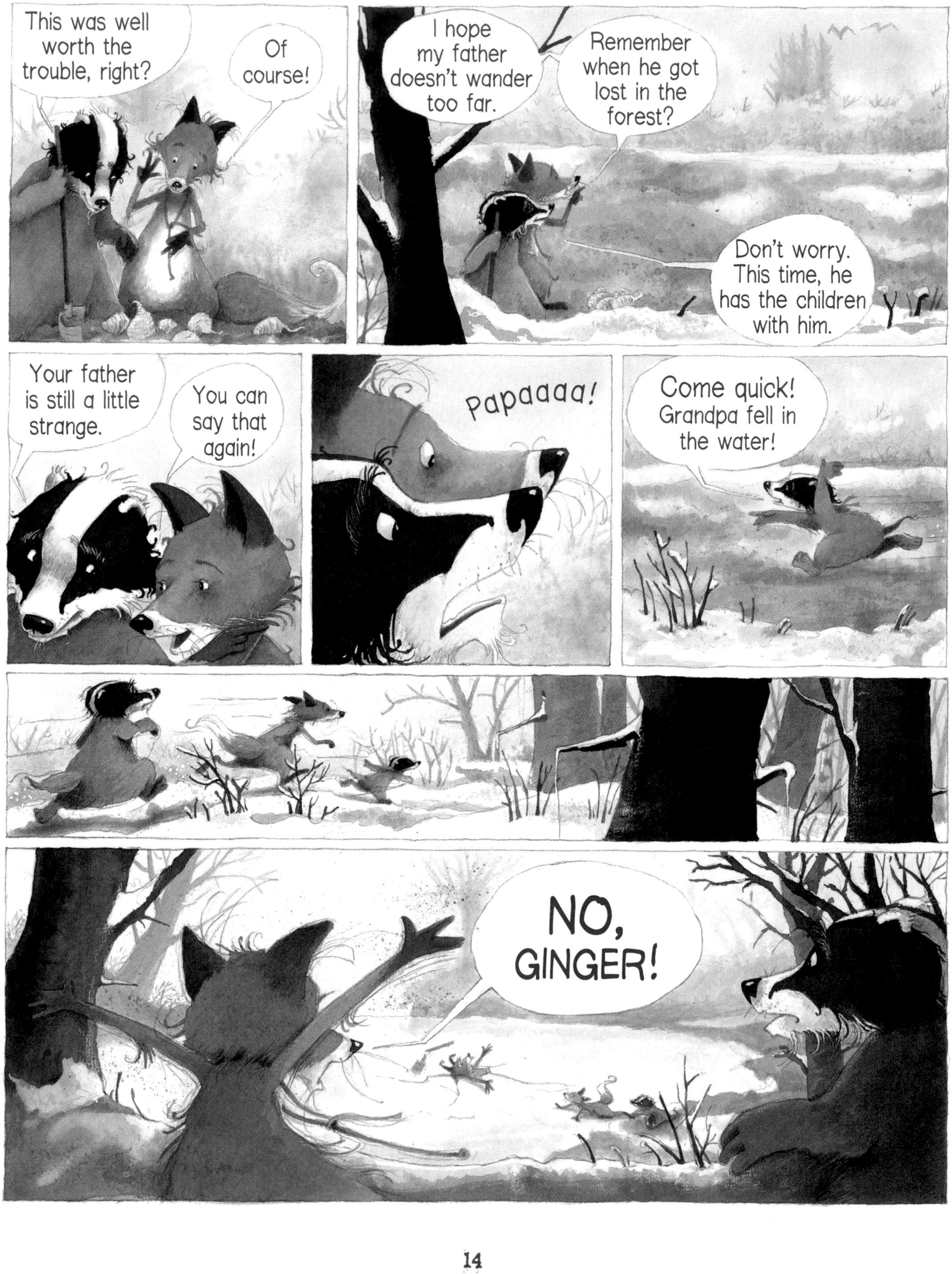
This was well worth the trouble, right?
Of course!
I hope my father doesn't wander too far.
Remember when he got lost in the forest?
Don't worry. This time, he has the children with him.
Your father is still a little strange.
You can say that again!
Papaaaa!
Come quick! Grandpa fell in the water!
NO, GINGER!

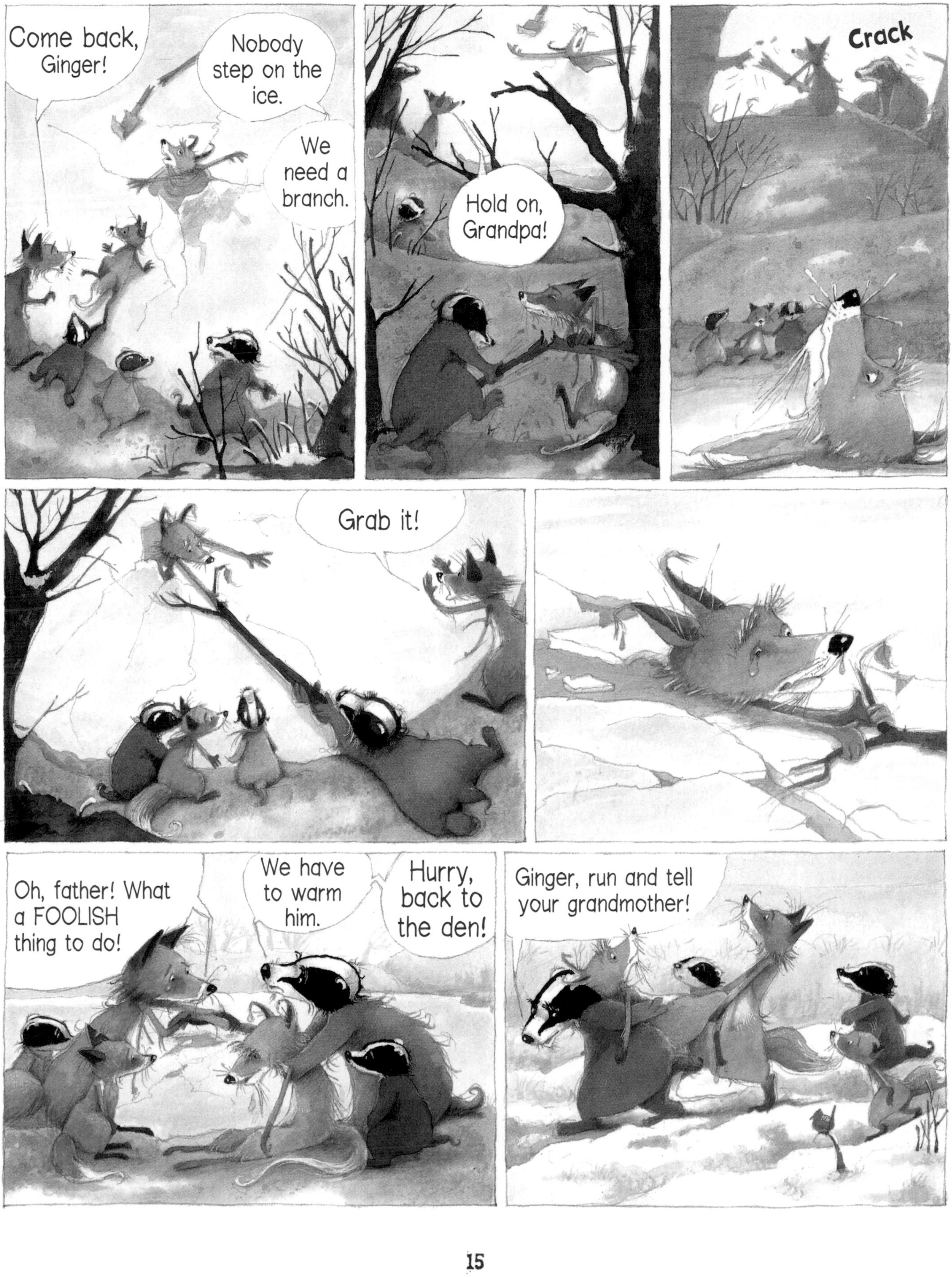
Come back, Ginger!
Nobody step on the ice.
We need a branch.
Hold on, Grandpa!
Crack
Grab it!
Oh, father! What a FOOLISH thing to do!
We have to warm him.
Hurry, back to the den!
Ginger, run and tell your grandmother!

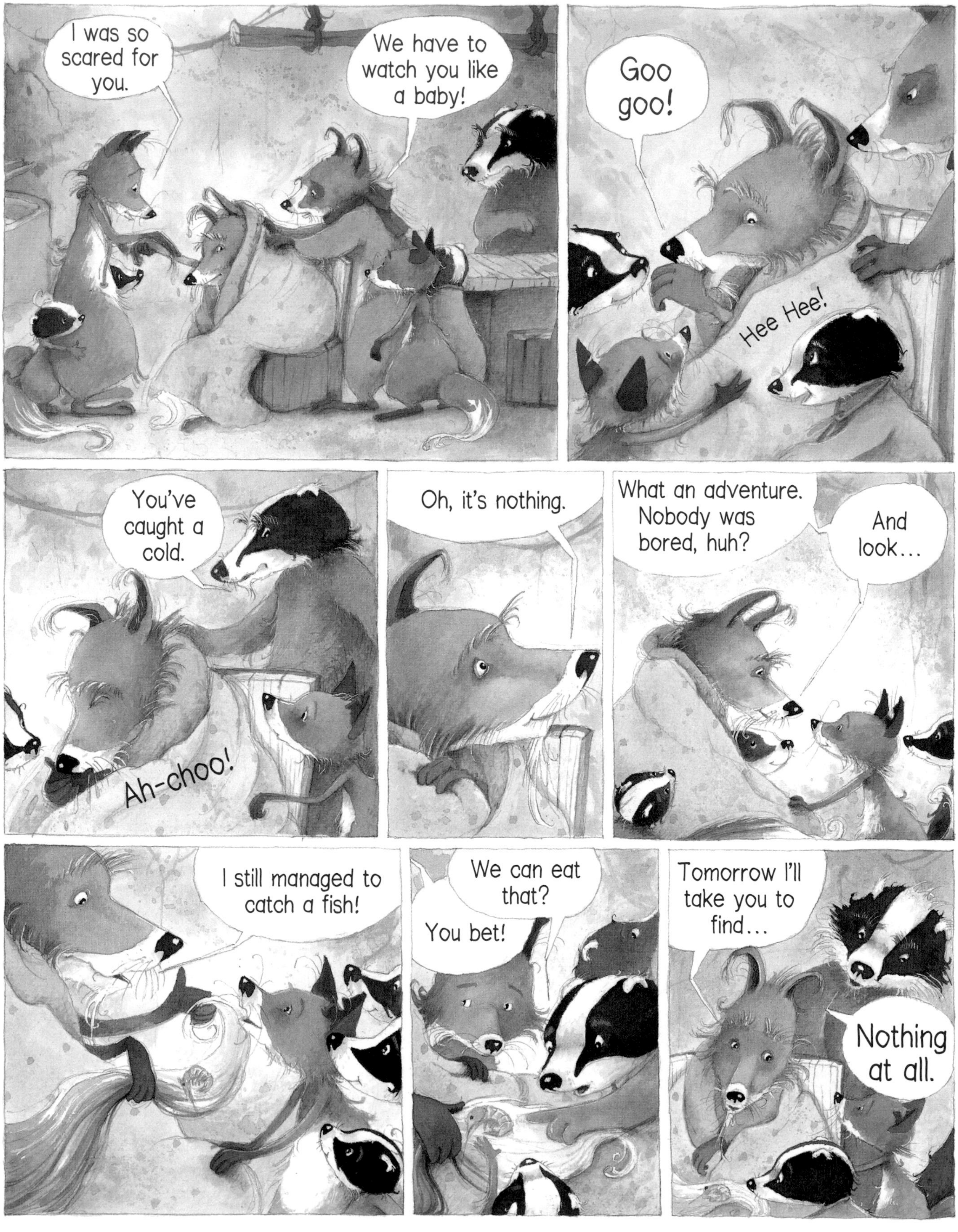
I was so scared for you.
We have to watch you like a baby!
Goo goo!
Hee Hee!
You've caught a cold.
Ah-choo!
Oh, it's nothing.
What an adventure. Nobody was bored, huh?
And look...
I still managed to catch a fish!
We can eat that?
You bet!
Tomorrow I'll take you to find...
Nothing at all.

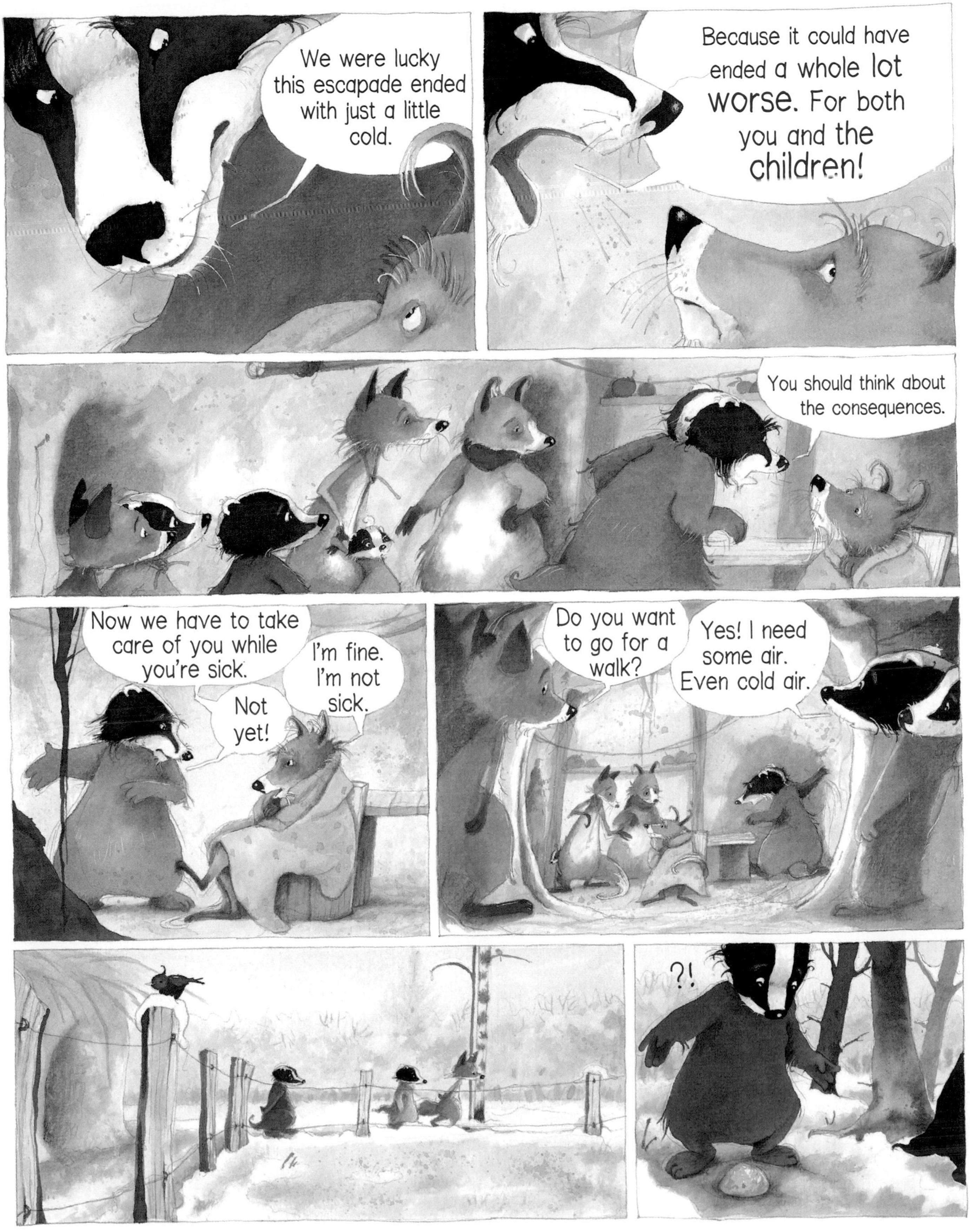
We were lucky this escapade ended with just a little cold.
Because it could have ended a whole lot worse. For both you and the children!
You should think about the consequences.
Now we have to take care of you while you're sick.
Not yet!
I'm fine. I'm not sick.
Do you want to go for a walk?
Yes! I need some air. Even cold air.
?!

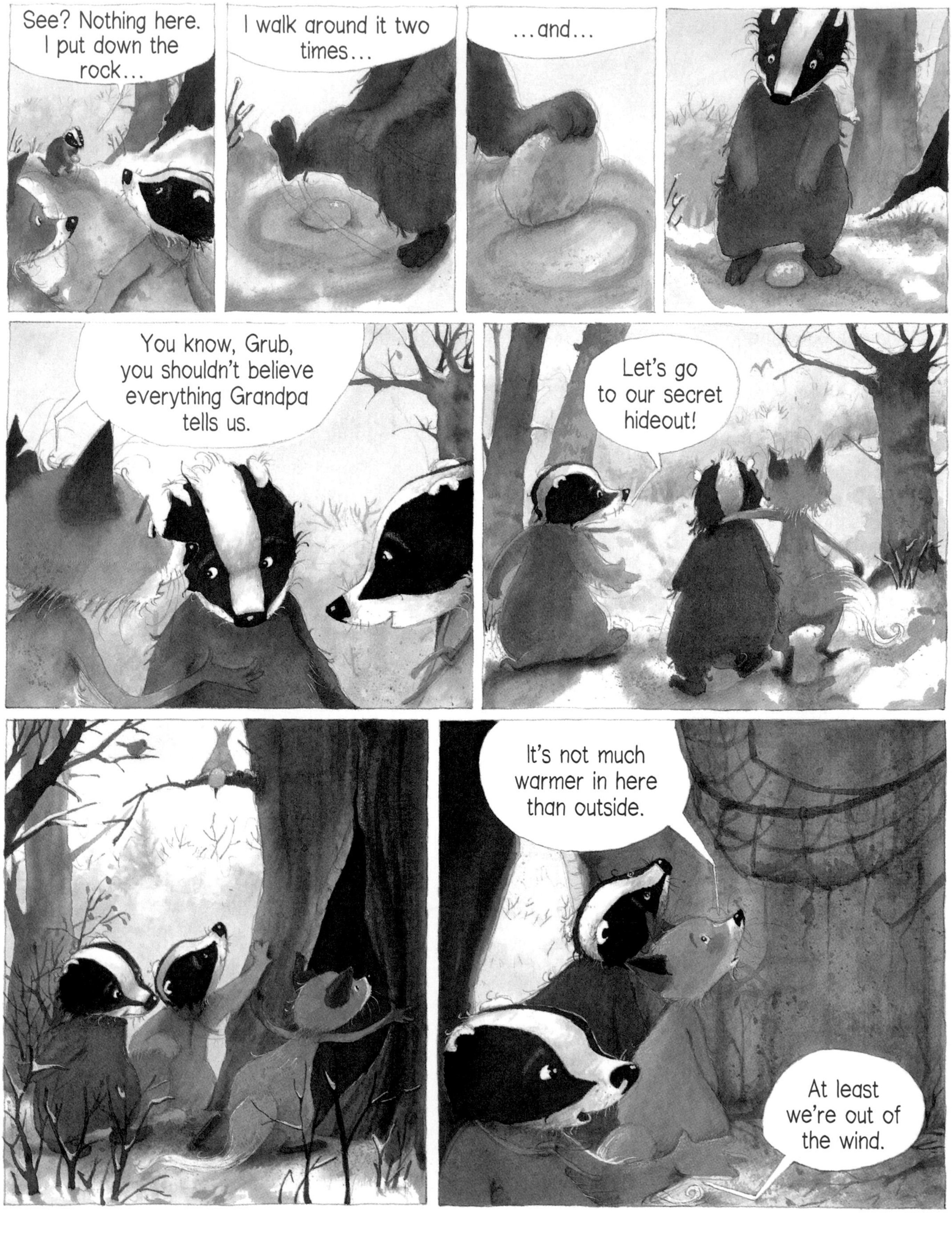
See? Nothing here. I put down the rock...
I walk around it two times...
...and...
You know, Grub, you shouldn't believe everything Grandpa tells us.
Let's go to our secret hideout!
It's not much warmer in here than outside.
At least we're out of the wind.

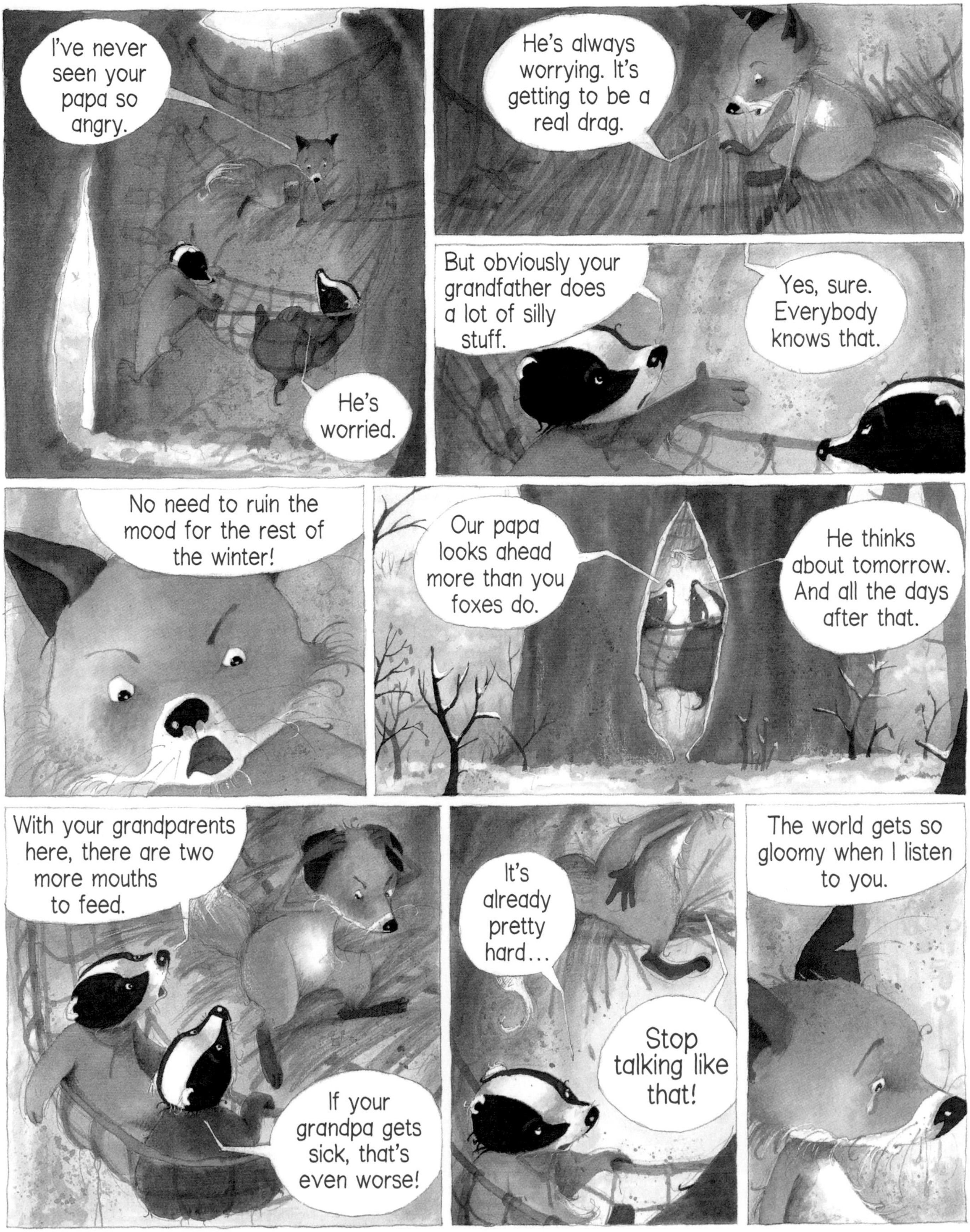
I've never seen your papa so angry.
He's worried.
He's always worrying. It's getting to be a real drag.
But obviously your grandfather does a lot of silly stuff.
Yes, sure. Everybody knows that.
No need to ruin the mood for the rest of the winter!
Our papa looks ahead more than you foxes do.
He thinks about tomorrow. And all the days after that.
With your grandparents here, there are two more mouths to feed.
If your grandpa gets sick, that's even worse!
It's already pretty hard...
Stop talking like that!
The world gets so gloomy when I listen to you.

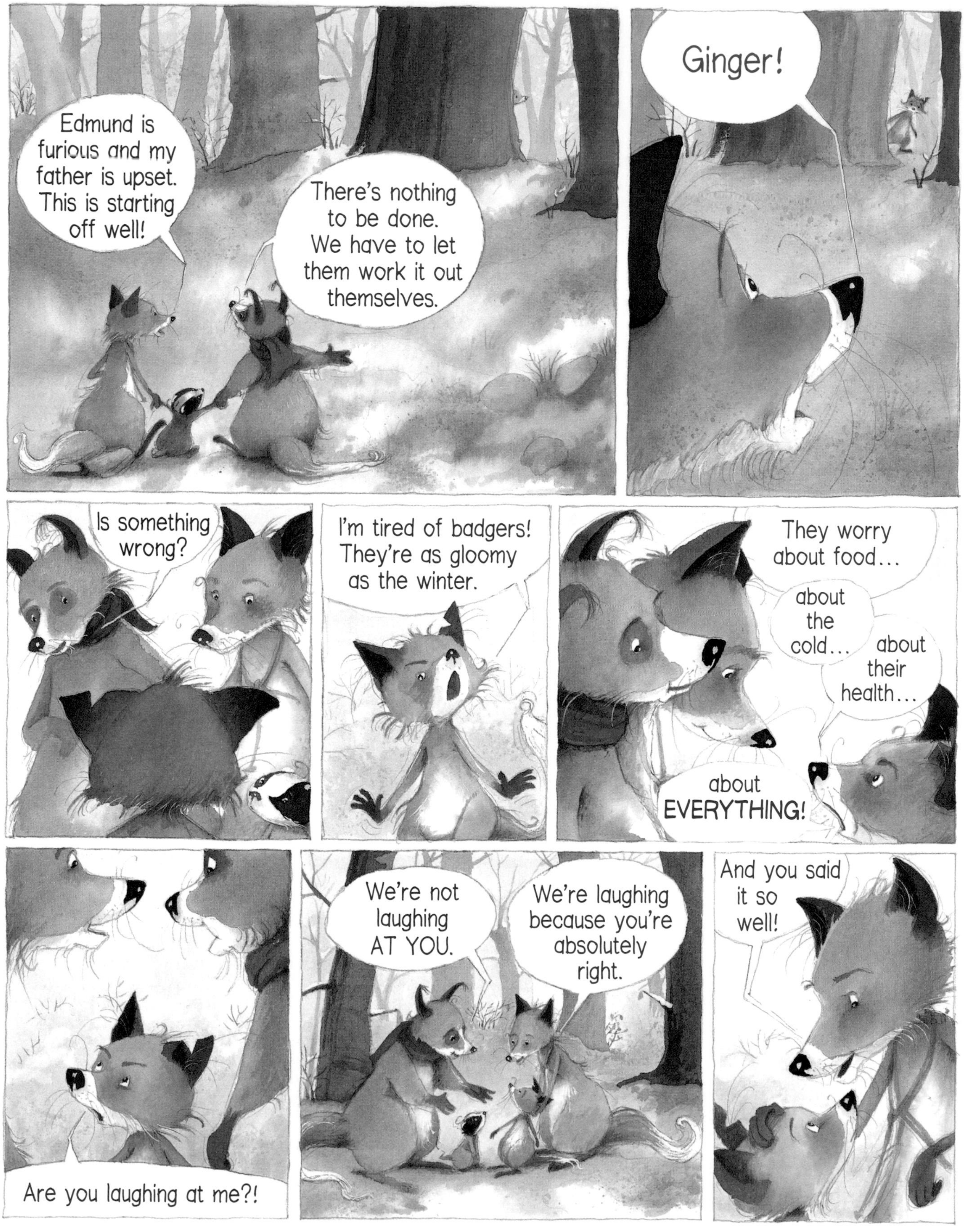
Edmund is furious and my father is upset. This is starting off well!
There's nothing to be done. We have to let them work it out themselves.
Ginger!
Is something wrong?
I'm tired of badgers! They're as gloomy as the winter.
They worry about food...
about the cold...
about their health...
about EVERYTHING!
Are you laughing at me?!
We're not laughing AT YOU.
We're laughing because you're absolutely right.
And you said it so well!

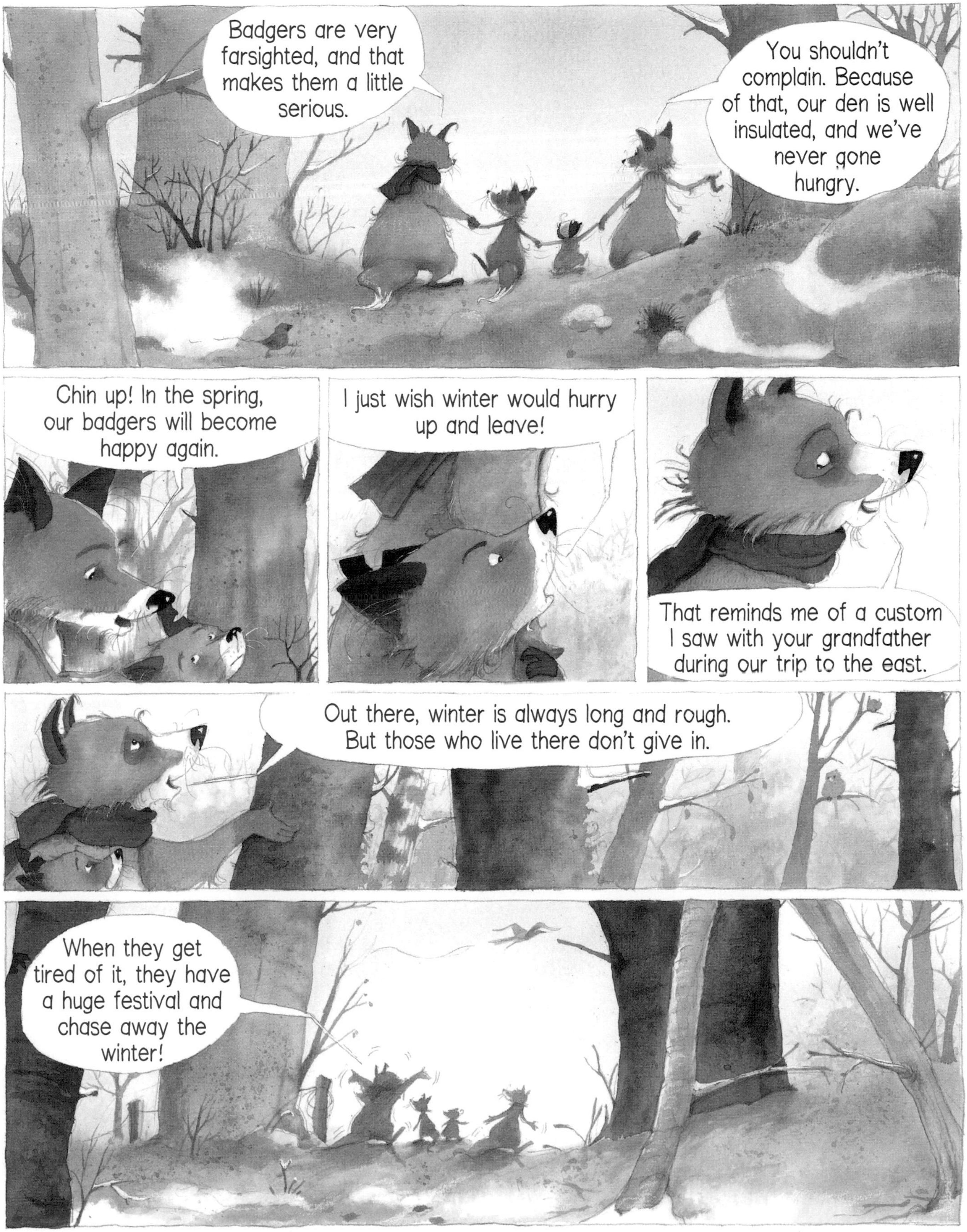

Badgers are very farsighted, and that makes them a little serious.
You shouldn't complain. Because of that, our den is well insulated, and we've never gone hungry.
Chin up! In the spring, our badgers will become happy again.
I just wish winter would hurry up and leave!
That reminds me of a custom I saw with your grandfather during our trip to the east.
Out there, winter is always long and rough. But those who live there don't give in.
When they get tired of it, they have a huge festival and chase away the winter!

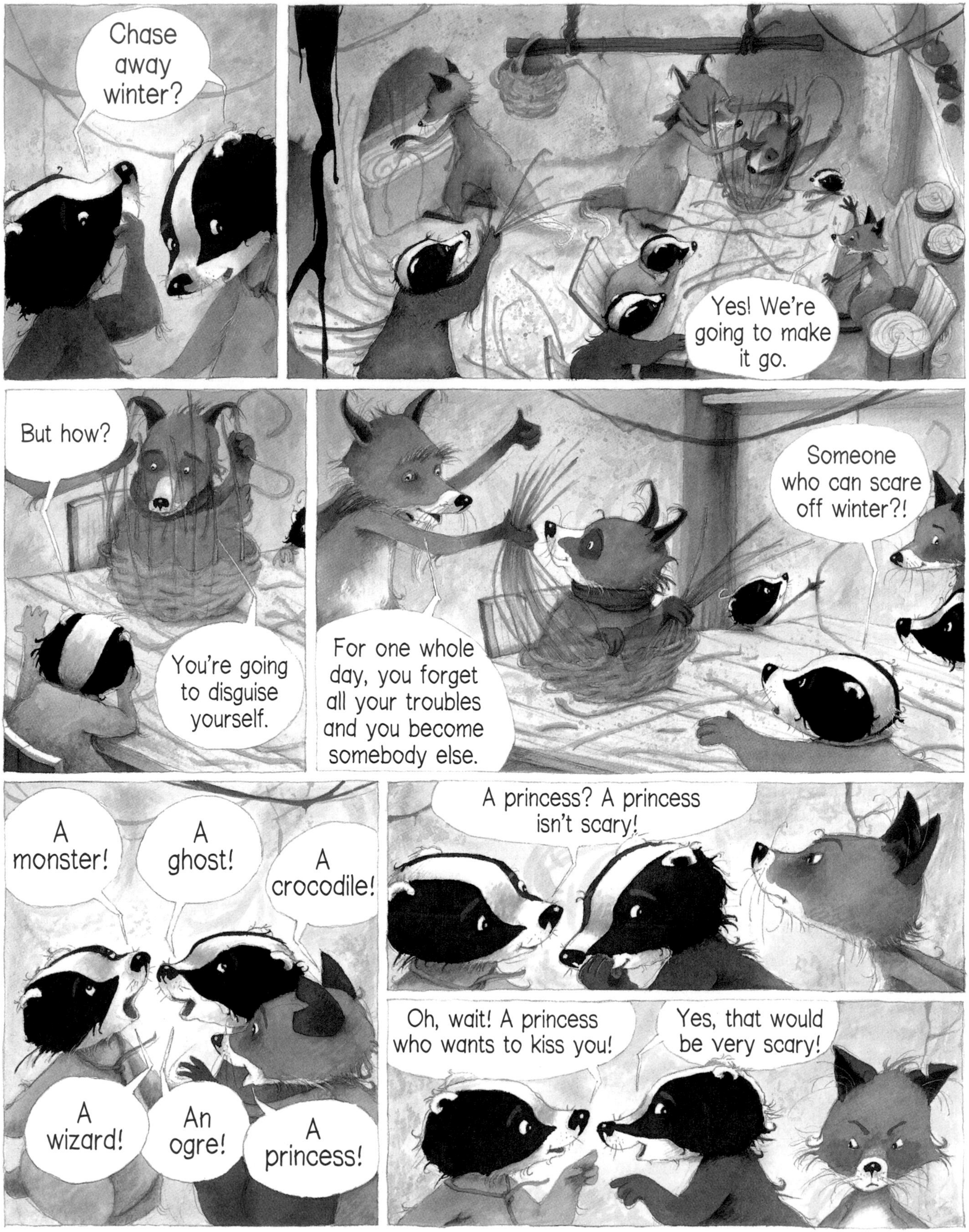
Chase away winter?
Yes! We're going to make it go.
But how?
You're going to disguise yourself.
For one whole day, you forget all your troubles and you become somebody else.
Someone who can scare off winter?!
A monster!
A ghost!
A crocodile!
A wizard!
An ogre!
A princess!
A princess? A princess isn't scary!
Oh, wait! A princess who wants to kiss you!
Yes, that would be very scary!

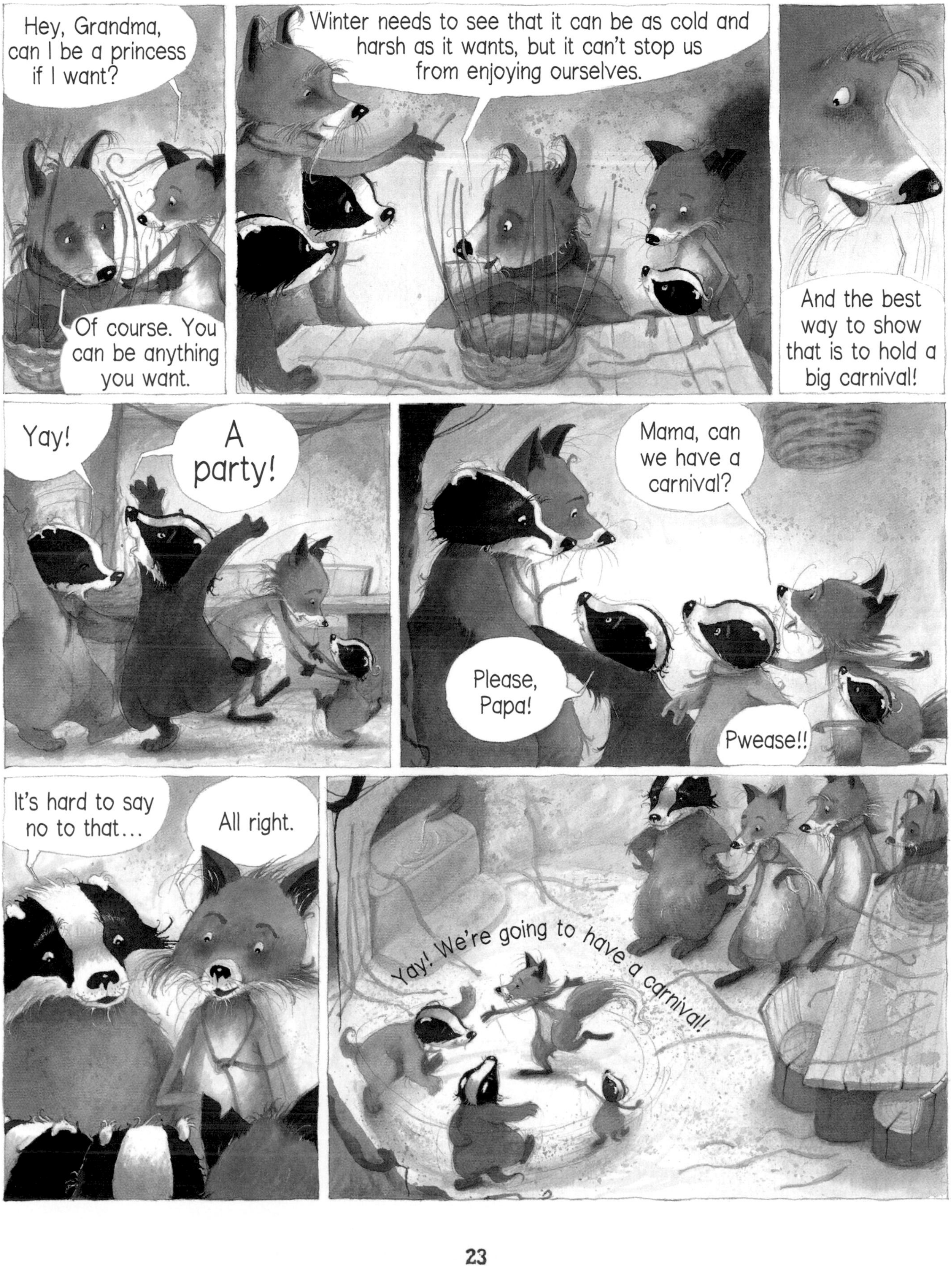

Hey, Grandma, can I be a princess if I want?
Of course. You can be anything you want.
Winter needs to see that it can be as cold and harsh as it wants, but it can't stop us from enjoying ourselves.
And the best way to show that is to hold a big carnival!
Yay!
A party!
Mama, can we have a carnival?
Please, Papa!
Pwease!!
It's hard to say no to that...
All right.
Yay! We're going to have a carnival!

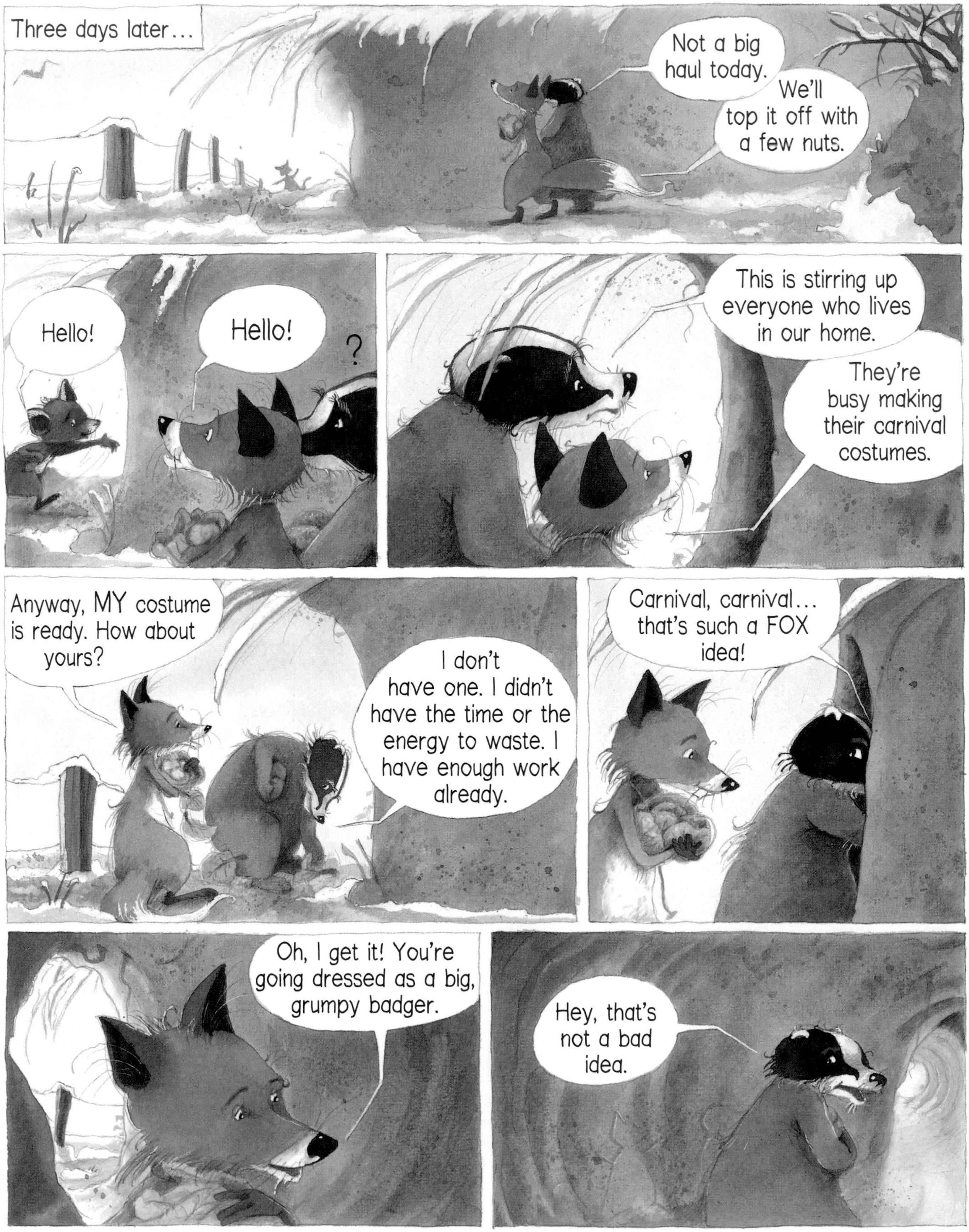
Three days later...
Not a big haul today.
We'll top it off with a few nuts.
Hello!
Hello!
?
This is stirring up everyone who lives in our home.
They're busy making their carnival costumes.
Anyway, MY costume is ready. How about yours?
I don't have one. I didn't have the time or the energy to waste. I have enough work already.
Carnival, carnival... that's such a FOX idea!
Oh, I get it! You're going dressed as a big, grumpy badger.
Hey, that's not a bad idea.

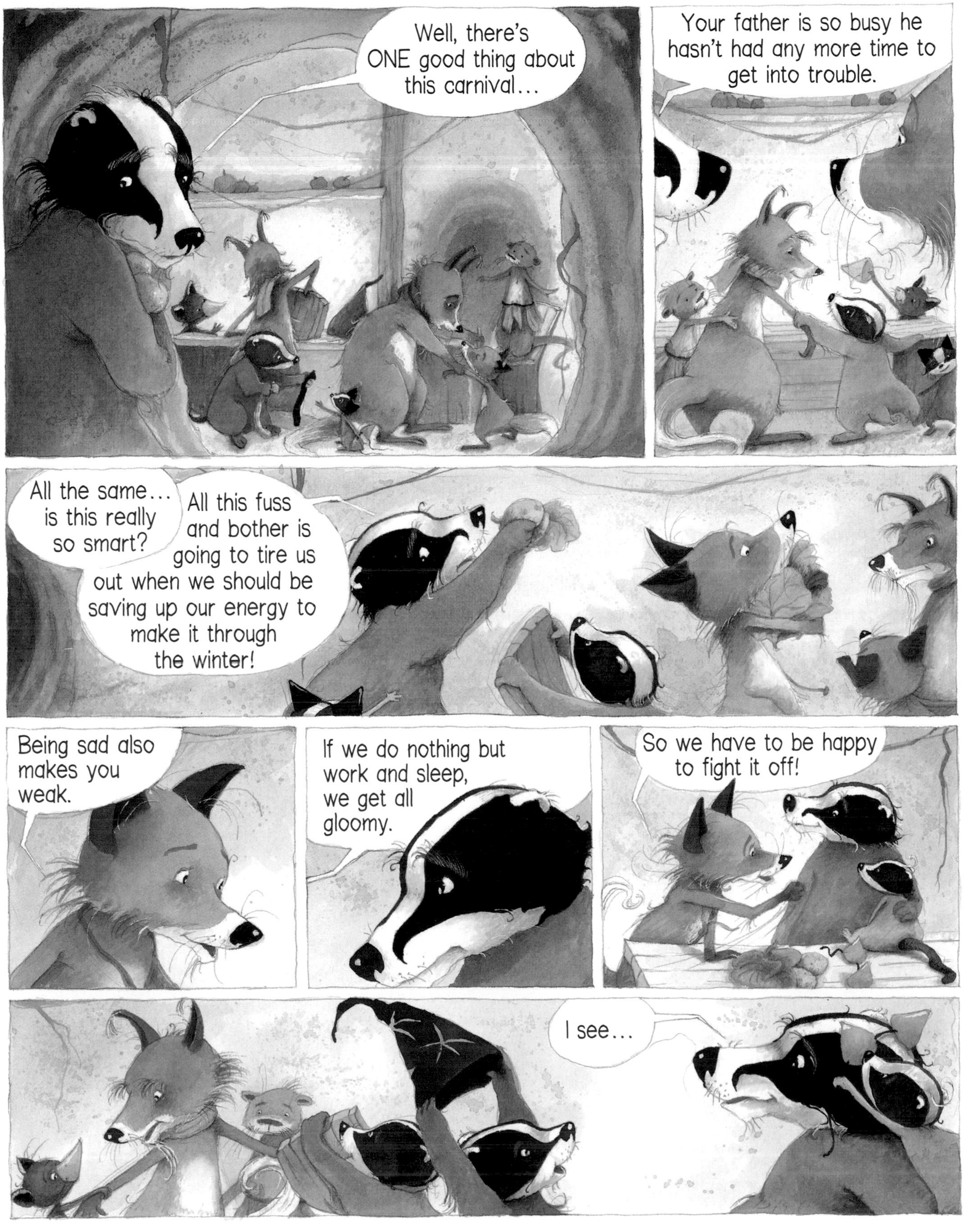

Well, there's ONE good thing about this carnival...
Your father is so busy he hasn't had any more time to get into trouble.
All the same... is this really so smart?
All this fuss and bother is going to tire us out when we should be saving up our energy to make it through the winter!
Being sad also makes you weak.
If we do nothing but work and sleep, we get all gloomy.
So we have to be happy to fight it off!
I see...

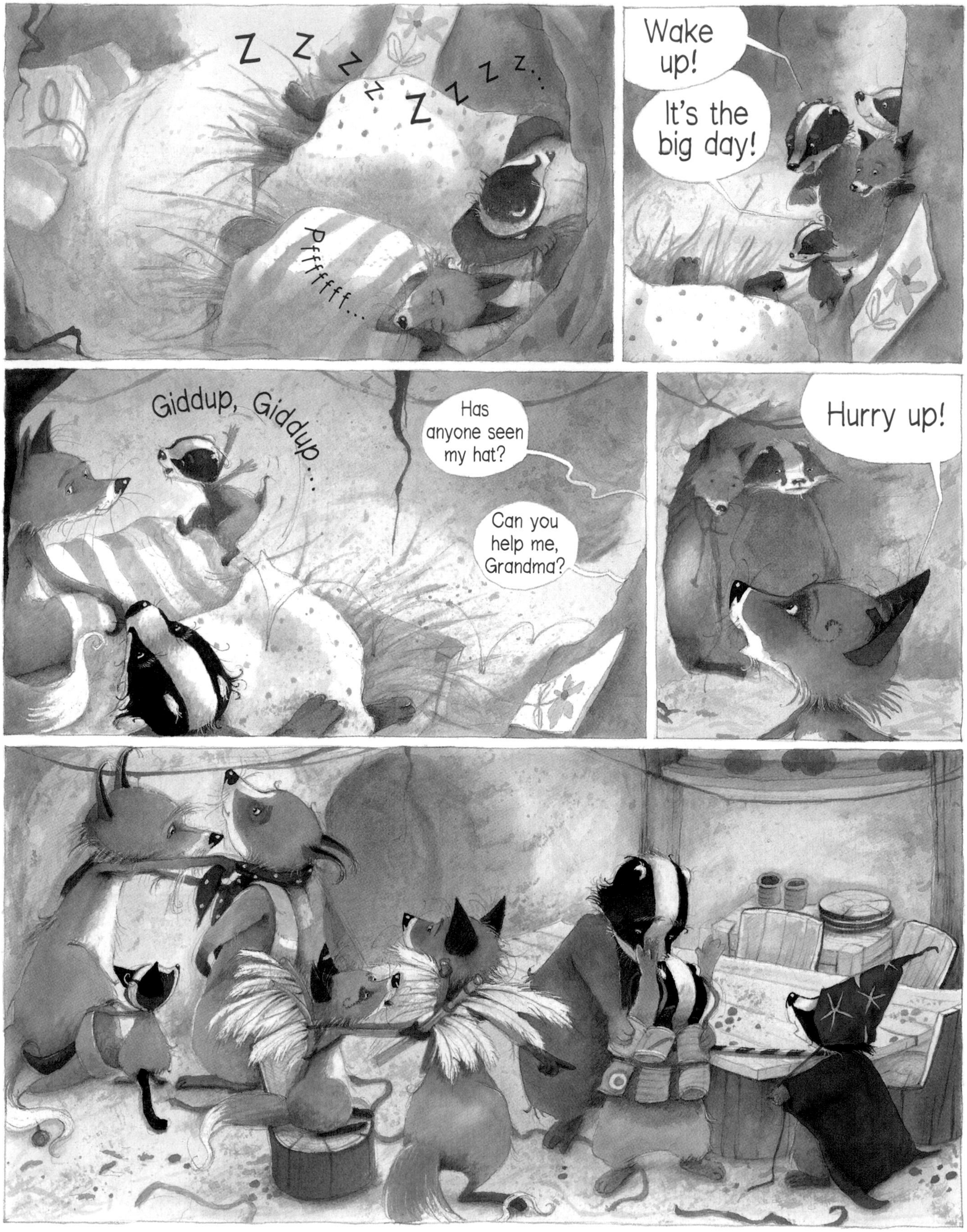
Z Z Z Z Z Z Z Z...
Pffffff...
Wake up!
It's the big day!
Giddup, Giddup...
Has anyone seen my hat?
Can you help me, Grandma?
Hurry up!

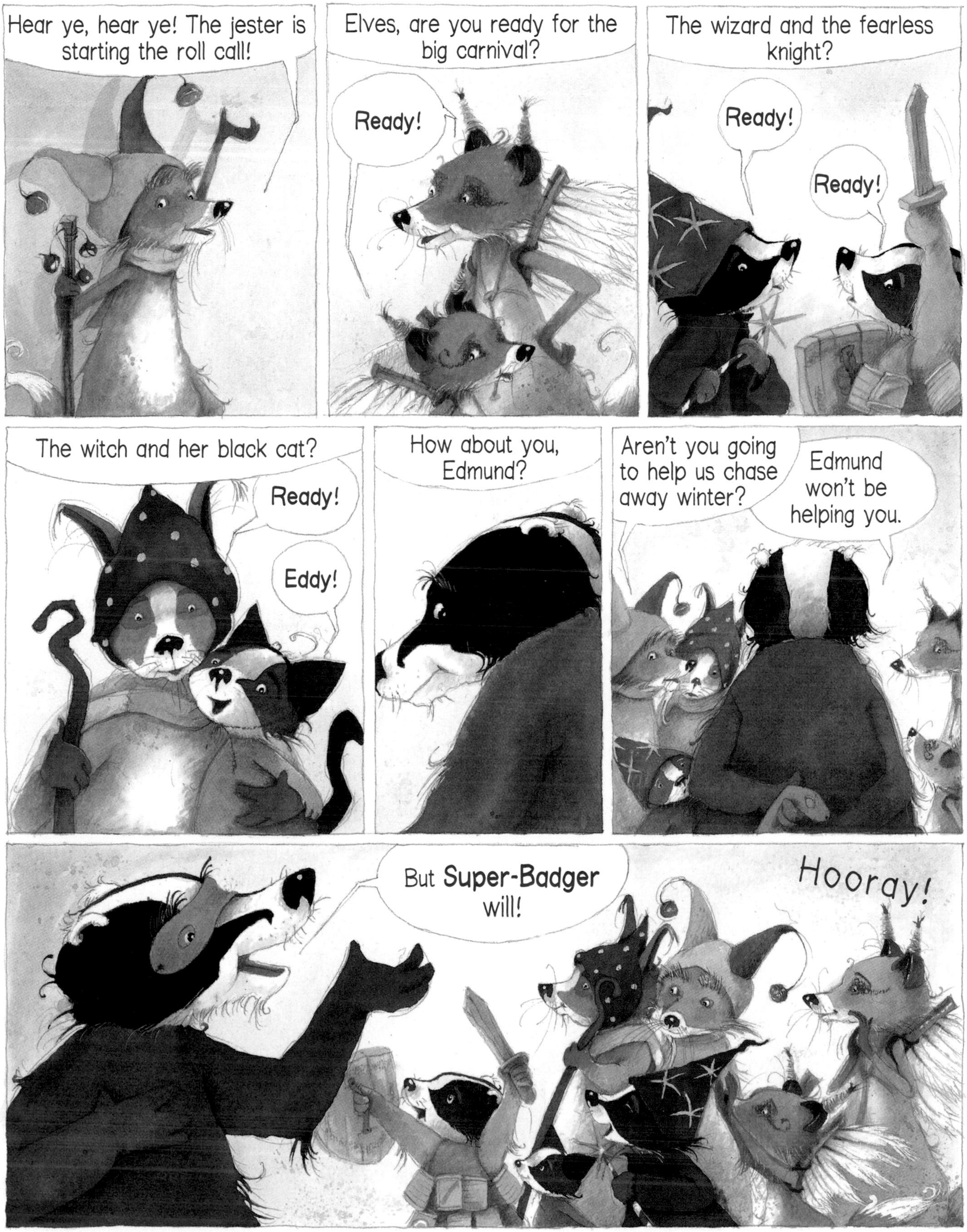
Hear ye, hear ye! The jester is starting the roll call!
Elves, are you ready for the big carnival?
Ready!
The wizard and the fearless knight?
Ready!
Ready!
The witch and her black cat?
Ready!
Eddy!
How about you, Edmund?
Aren't you going to help us chase away winter?
Edmund won't be helping you.
But **Super-Badger** will!
Hooray!

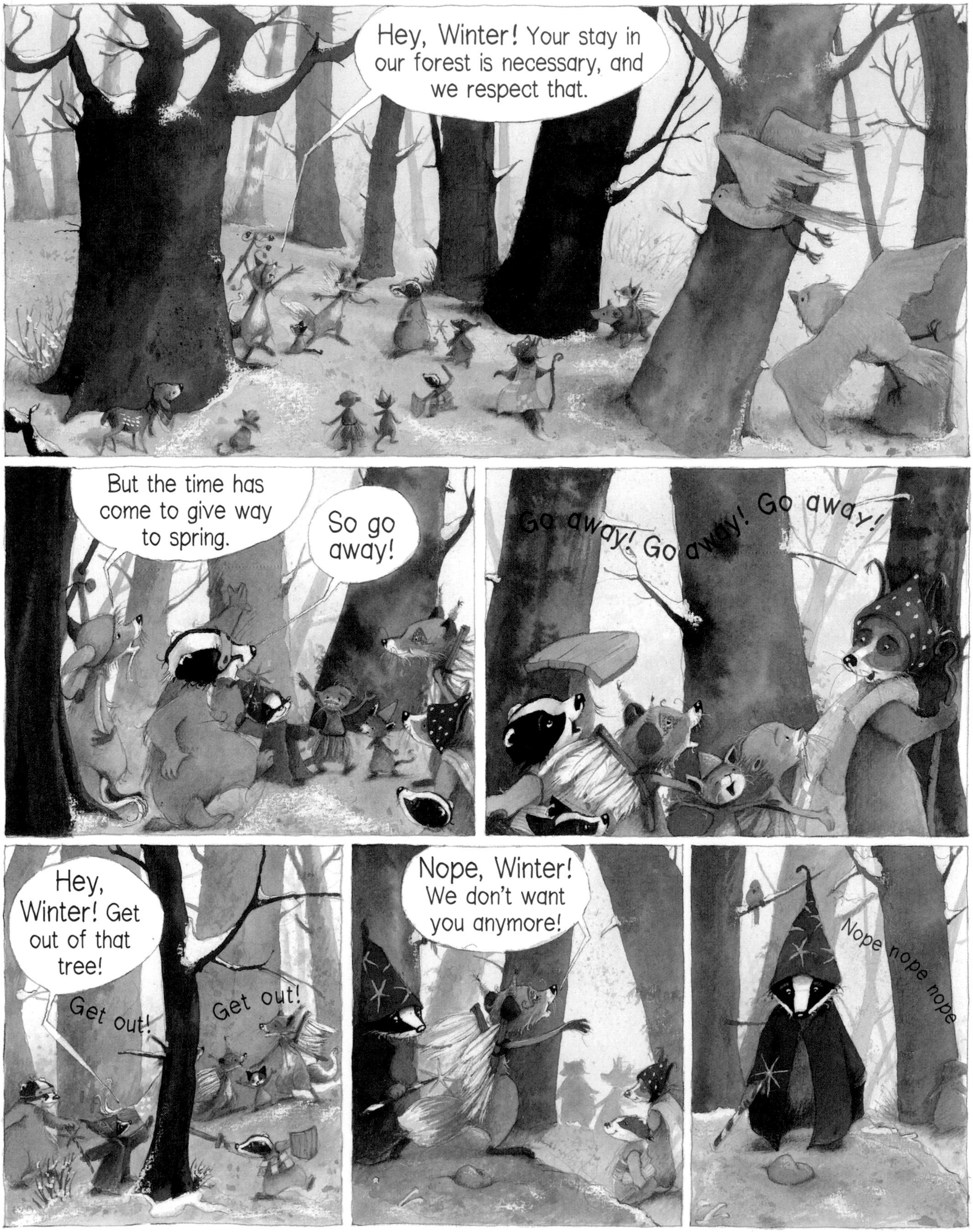
Hey, Winter! Your stay in our forest is necessary, and we respect that.
But the time has come to give way to spring.
So go away!
Go away! Go away! Go away!
Hey, Winter! Get out of that tree!
Get out!
Get out!
Nope, Winter! We don't want you anymore!
Nope nope nope

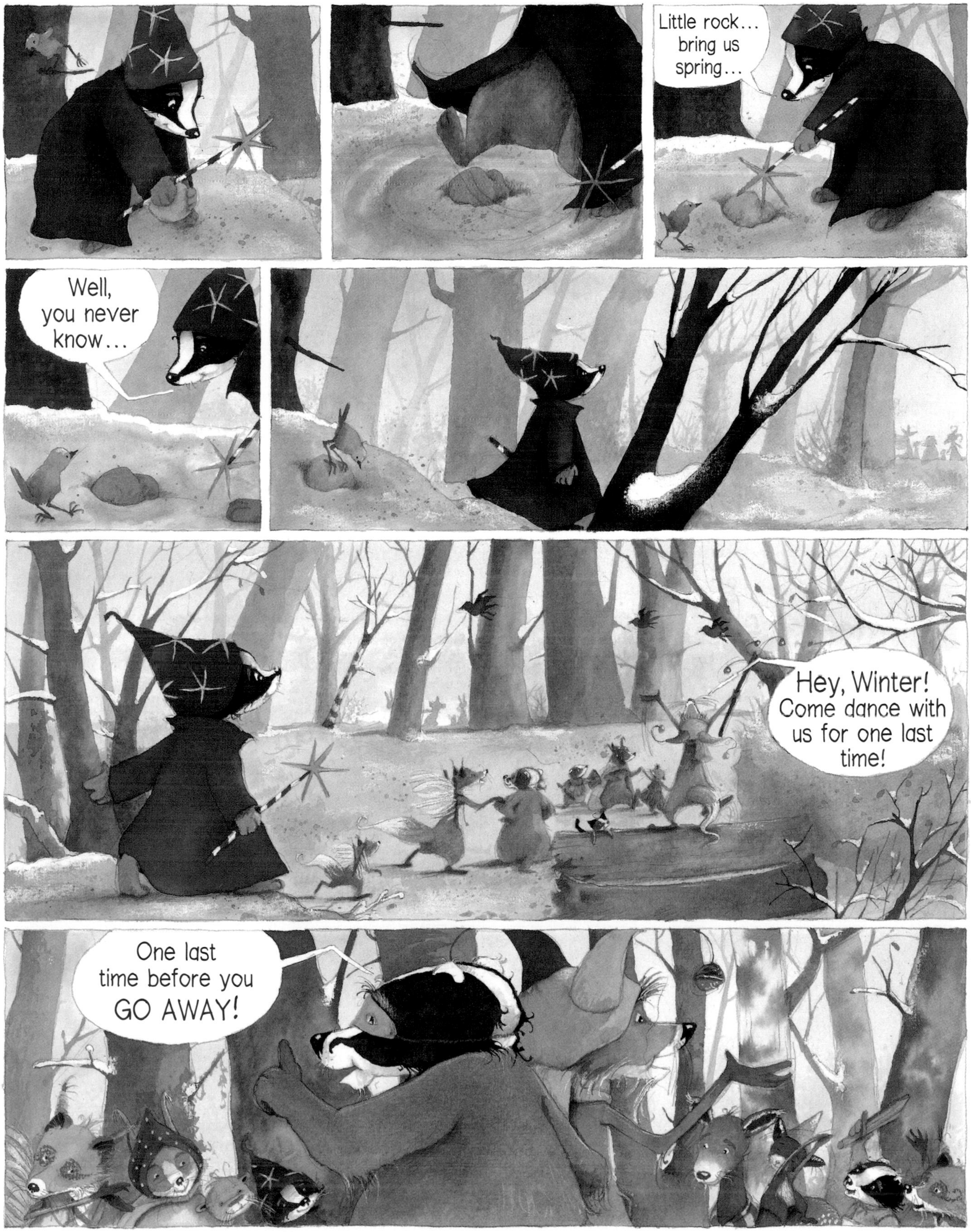
Little rock... bring us spring...
Well, you never know...
Hey, Winter! Come dance with us for one last time!
One last time before you GO AWAY!

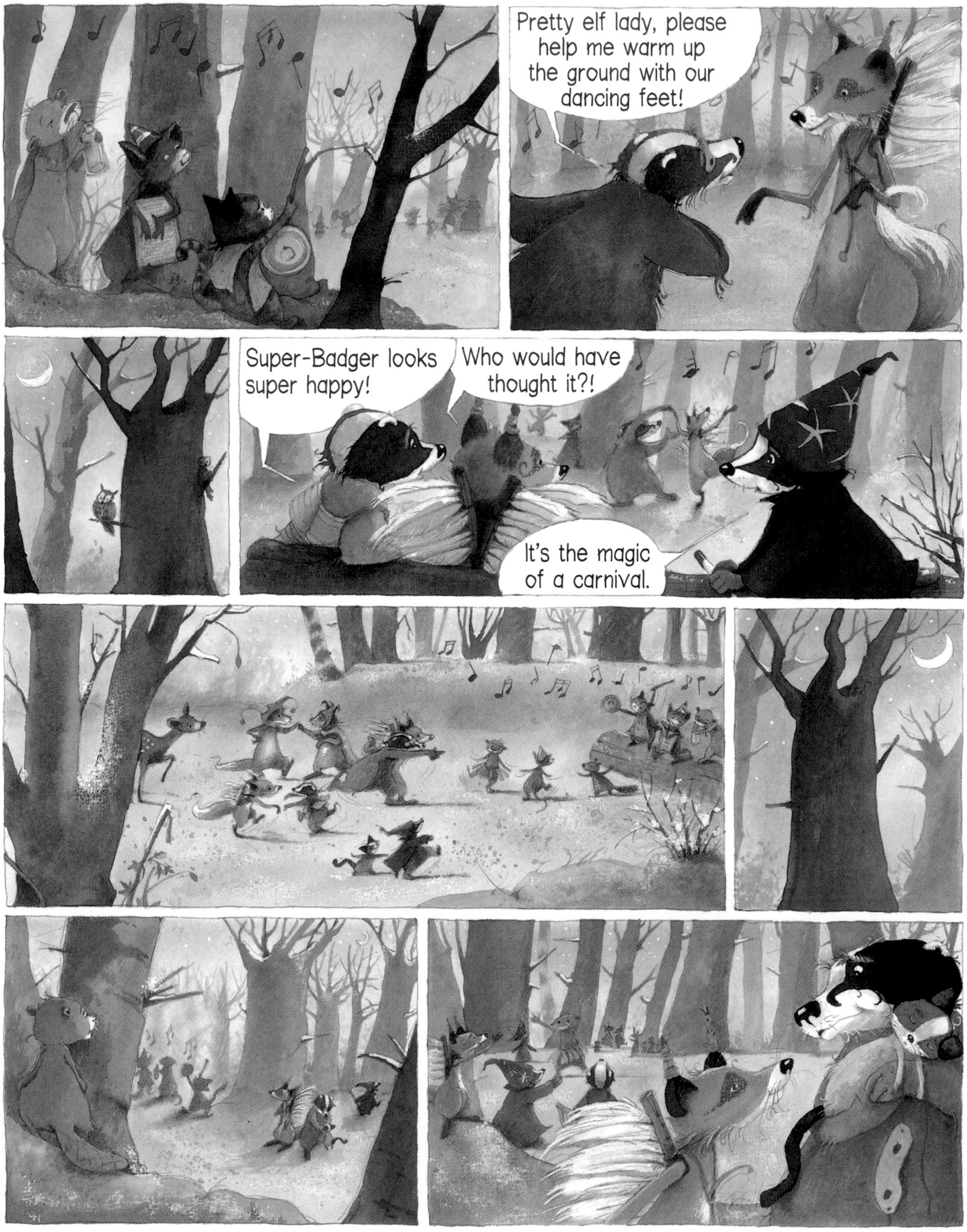
Pretty elf lady, please help me warm up the ground with our dancing feet!
Super-Badger looks super happy!
Who would have thought it?!
It's the magic of a carnival.

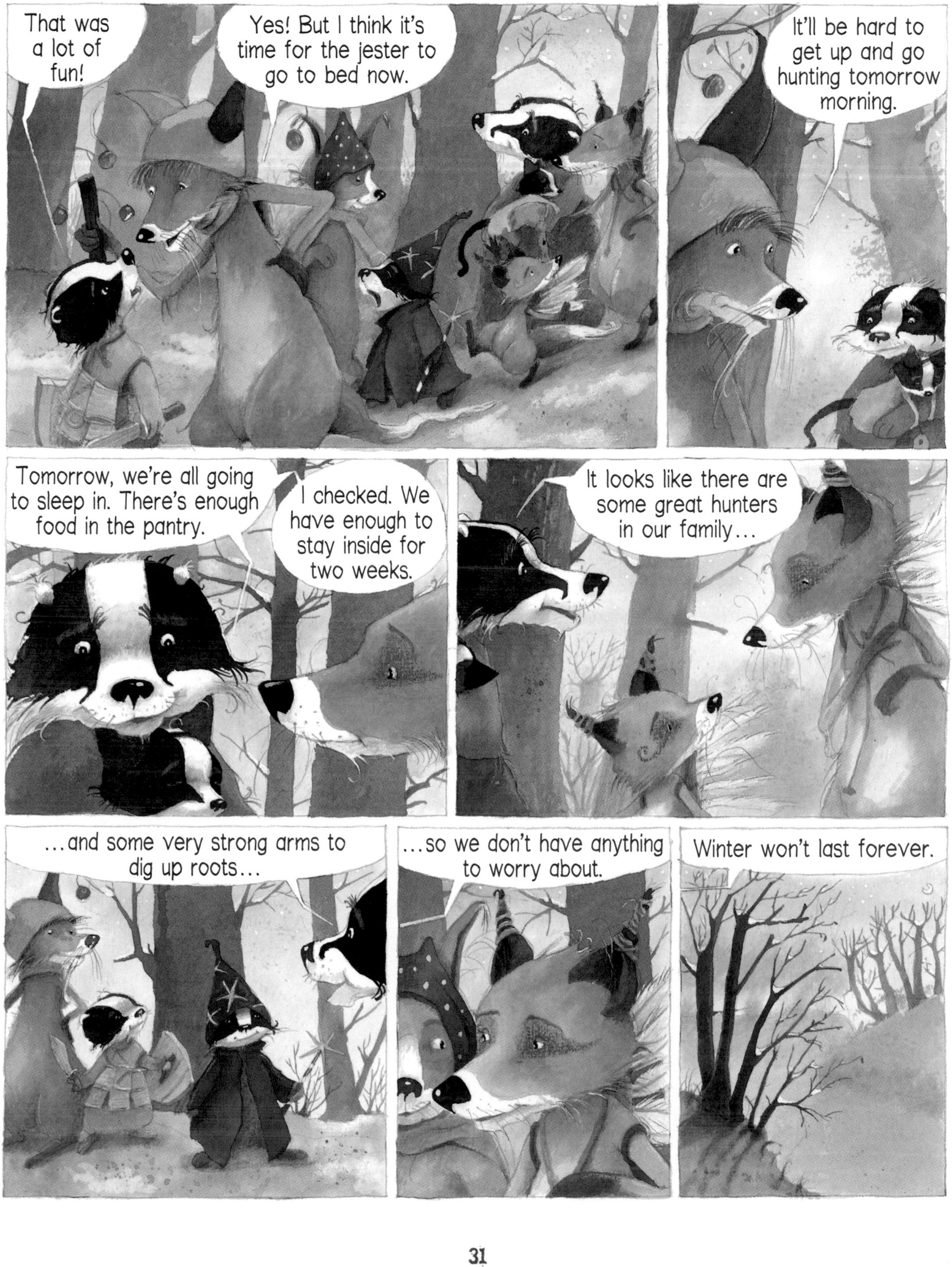
That was a lot of fun!
Yes! But I think it's time for the jester to go to bed now.
It'll be hard to get up and go hunting tomorrow morning.
Tomorrow, we're all going to sleep in. There's enough food in the pantry.
I checked. We have enough to stay inside for two weeks.
It looks like there are some great hunters in our family...
...and some very strong arms to dig up roots...
...so we don't have anything to worry about.
Winter won't last forever.

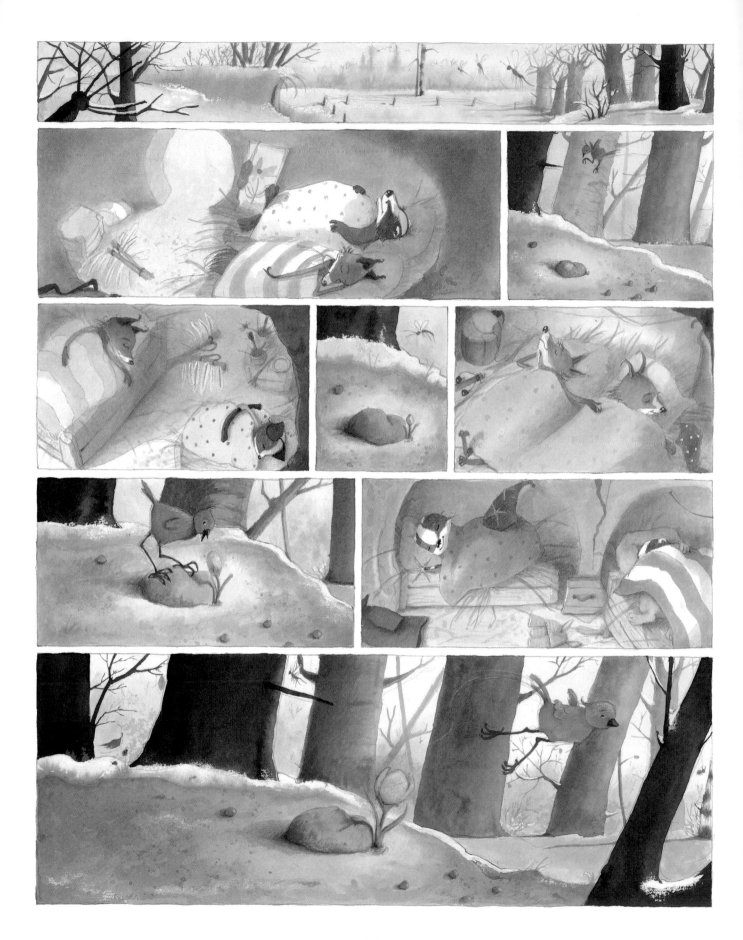

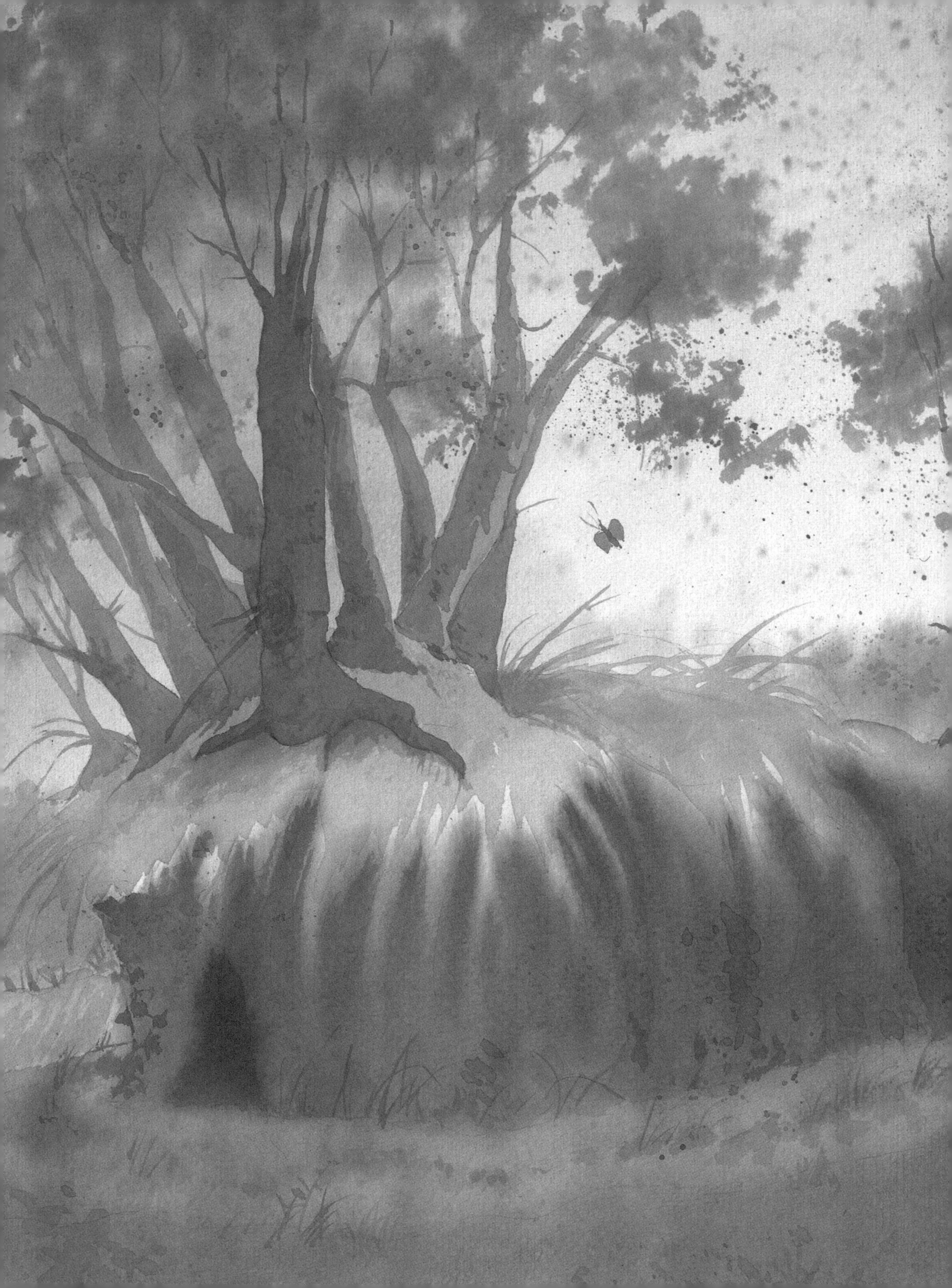

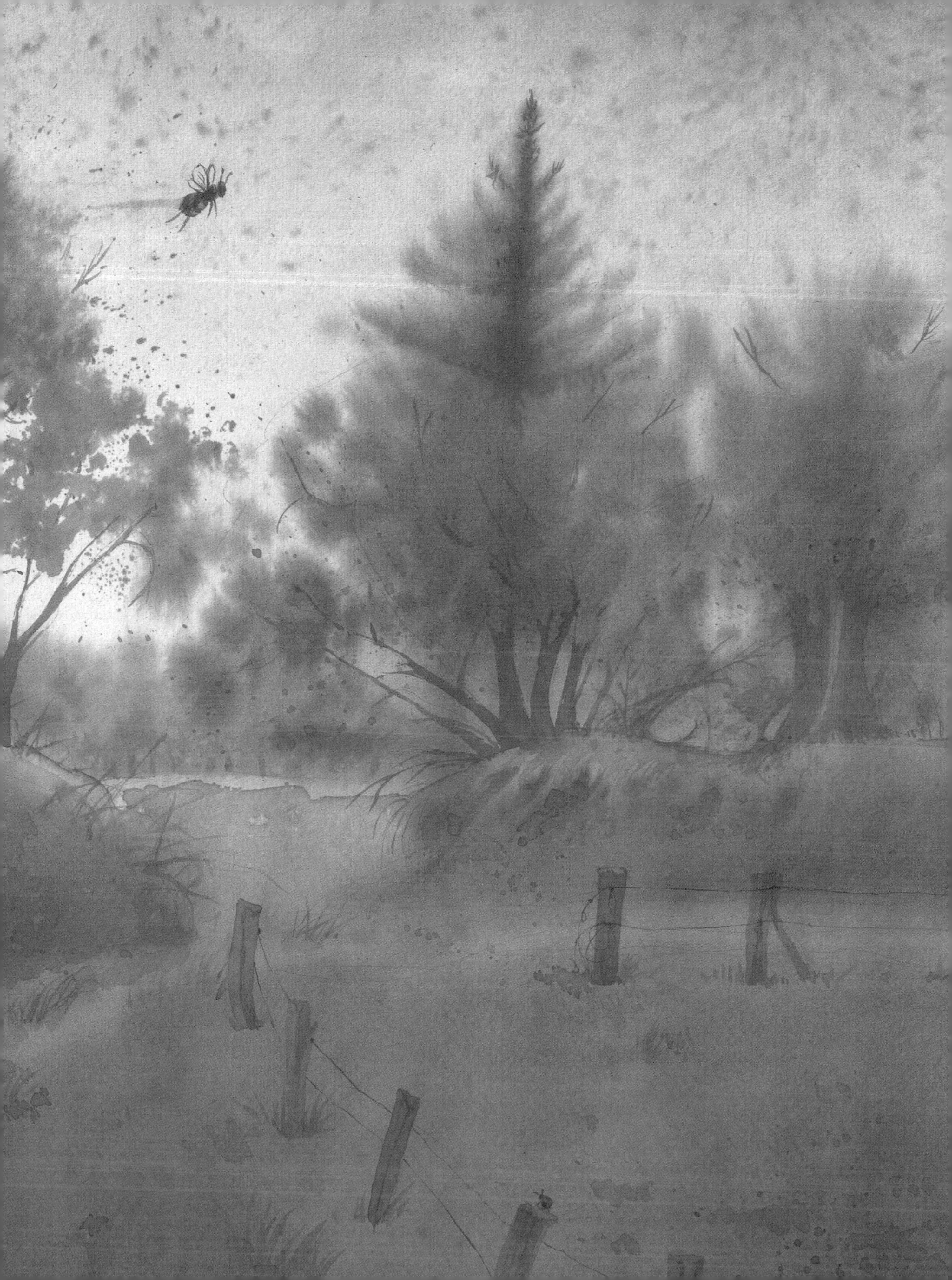